CAPTIVE IN
HIS CASTLE

CAPTIVE IN HIS CASTLE

BY

CHANTELLE SHAW

First published in Great Britain 2013
by Mills & Boon, an imprint of Harlequin (UK) Limited.
Large Print edition 2013
Harlequin (UK) Limited, Eton House,
18-24 Paradise Road, Richmond, Surrey TW9 1SR

© Chantelle Shaw 2013

ISBN: 978 0 263 23220 2

Harlequin (UK) policy is to use papers that are natural,
renewable and recyclable products and made from
wood grown in sustainable forests. The logging and
manufacturing process conform to the legal environmental
regulations of the country of origin.

Printed and bound in Great Britain
by CPI Antony Rowe, Chippenham, Wiltshire

CHAPTER ONE

'*WHO THE HELL is Jess?*'

Drago Cassari raked his fingers through the swathe of dark hair that had fallen forward onto his brow, concern and frustration etched onto his hard features as he stared at the motionless figure of his cousin lying in the bed in the intensive care unit. Angelo's face was grey against the white sheets. Only the almost imperceptible rise and fall of his chest indicated that he was still clinging to life, aided by the various tubes attached to his body, while the machine next to the bed recorded his vital signs.

At least he was now breathing unaided, and three days after he had been pulled from the wreckage of his car and rushed to the Venice-Mestre hospital there were indications that he was beginning to regain consciousness. He had even muttered something. Just one word. A name.

'Do you know who Angelo is referring to?' Drago turned his gaze on the two women who were standing at the end of the bed, clinging to each other and weeping. 'Is Jess a friend of Angelo's?'

His aunt Dorotea gave a sob. 'I don't know what his involvement with her is. You know how strangely he has been behaving lately. He hardly ever answered his phone when I called him. But I did manage to speak to him a few days before...' her voice shook '...before the accident, and he told me that he had given up his college course and was living with a woman called Jess Harper.'

'Then perhaps she is his mistress.' Drago was not overly surprised to hear that his cousin had dropped out of the business course he had been studying at a private London college. Angelo had been overindulged by his mother since his father's death when he had been a young boy, and he shied away from anything that approached hard work. Rather more surprising was the news that he had been living with a woman in England. Angelo was painfully lacking in self-confidence with the opposite sex, but it sounded as though he had overcome his shyness.

'Did he give you the address of where he was staying? I need to contact this woman and arrange for her to visit him.' Drago glanced across the bed to the expert neurologist who was in charge of his cousin's care. 'Do you think there is a chance that the sound of her voice might rouse Angelo?'

'It is possible,' the doctor replied cautiously. 'If your cousin has a close relationship with this woman then he might respond if she talks to him.'

Aunt Dorotea gave another sob. 'I'm not sure it would be a good idea to bring her here. I am afraid she is a bad influence on Angelo.'

Drago frowned. 'What do you mean? Surely if this Jess Harper can help to rouse him then it is imperative that she comes to Italy as soon as possible? Why do you think she is a bad influence?'

He controlled his impatience as his aunt collapsed onto a chair and wept so hard that her shoulders shook. His jaw clenched. He understood her agony. When he had first seen Angelo after he had undergone surgery to stem the bleed in his brain Drago had felt the acid burn of tears at the back of his throat. His cousin was just twenty-two, in many ways still a boy—although when *he* had been that age he had already become chairman of Cassa di Cassari, with a great weight of responsibility and expectation on his shoulders, he remembered. The deaths of his father and uncle, who had been killed in an avalanche while they were skiing, had thrust Drago into the cut-throat world of big business. He had also had to take care of his devastated mother and aunt, and he had assumed the role of a father figure to his then seven-year-old cousin.

Seeing Angelo like this tore at his insides. The waiting, the wondering if the young man would be left with permanent brain damage, was torture. Drago was a man of action, a man used to being in control of every situation, but for the past three days he had felt helpless. His aunt and his mother were distraught, and he wished he could comfort them and assure them that Angelo would recover. For the past fifteen years he had done his best to look after his family, and he hated the feeling that in this situation he was powerless. He had no magic wand to bring Angelo back to consciousness, but he had the name of a woman who might be able to help.

His mother was gently patting her sister-in-law's shoulder. 'Dorotea, you must tell Drago what Angelo has done, and why you are so worried about his involvement with the English-woman.'

Drago stared at his aunt. 'What *has* he done?'

For a few moments she did not answer, but at last she choked back her sobs. 'He has given this woman money…a lot of money. In fact all of the inheritance that his father left him,' Aunt Dorotea said in wavering voice. 'And that's not all. Jess Harper has a criminal record.'

'How do you know this?'

'A week ago Maurio Rochas, who used to be in charge of Angelo's trust fund and still acts as his financial adviser, phoned me. He was troubled because what he had to tell me was confidential information, but he felt I should know that Angelo had withdrawn his entire inheritance fund from the bank. When I spoke to Angelo I asked him what he had done with the money. He was very abrupt with me,' Aunt Dorotea explained in a hurt voice. 'It was most unlike him. But he finally admitted that he had lent his inheritance fund to this woman—Jess Harper—but he did not say why she needed the money, or when it would be repaid.'

Drago knew that the bulk of his cousin's inheritance was tied up in shares and other investments, but Angelo still had a huge fortune available to him—which he had apparently handed over to a woman who had a criminal record. It was not surprising Aunt Dorotea was concerned.

'Angelo was very cagey,' she continued. 'I felt he was hiding something from me. I was so worried that I phoned Maurio back to discuss the matter. Maurio admitted that out of concern for Angelo he had tried to find out more about this Englishwoman and had discovered that she was convicted of fraud some years ago.'

Drago swore softly and received a reproachful glance from his mother. *Dio!* He could not help feeling frustrated. Sometimes he wondered if his relatives would ever take charge of their own lives instead of relying on him to deal with their problems. He had encouraged his cousin to go to England to study, believing that it would do him good to be more independent. But it sounded as though Angelo had walked straight into trouble.

'What has the damned idiot done?' he muttered beneath his breath.

Unfortunately his aunt had excellent hearing.

'How can you blame Angelo? Especially when his life hangs in the balance?' she said tearfully. 'Perhaps this Jess Harper told Angelo some sob story that he fell for. You know what a soft heart he has. He is young, and I admit a little naïve. But I'm sure you remember how *you* were conned by that Russian woman years ago, Drago. Although of course that situation was a lot worse, because your actions almost forced Cassa di Cassari into bankruptcy.'

Drago gritted his teeth at his aunt's reminder of the most humiliating episode of his life. When he had been Angelo's age his judgement had been compromised by a woman's beautiful face and sexy body. He had fallen hard for the sensual promise in Natalia Yenka's dark eyes, and he had persuaded the board members of Cassa di Cassari—the luxury homeware company that had been founded by his great-grandfather—to make a huge investment in the Russian woman's business venture. But the venture had been a scam, and the catastrophic financial loss incurred by Cassa di Cassari had resulted in Drago only narrowly escaping a vote of no confidence from the board.

Since then he had worked hard to win back their support, and he was proud that under his leadership Cassa di Cassari had grown to be one of Italy's highest-grossing businesses, with a global export market. At the recent AGM he had announced that the company would be floated on the stockmarket for a record opening share price that would raise several billion pounds. It had been Drago's crowning moment—one that he had striven for with ruthless determination—but neither the board members nor his family knew of the personal sacrifices he had made in the pursuit of success, or of the emptiness inside him.

He shook his head as if to dismiss his thoughts, although dark memories of his past lingered in the shadows of his mind. Focusing his attention once more on his cousin, he felt a sharp pain, as if a knife blade had been thrust between his ribs. He did not think his aunt would cope if she lost her only son. This desperate waiting and hoping was intolerable, and if there was even the slightest chance that hearing the Englishwoman's voice would bring Angelo back from the abyss then Drago was convinced that he must persuade her to come to the hospital.

'Where are you going?' his aunt asked tremulously as he swung away from the bed and strode across the room.

'To find Jess Harper. And when I do you can be sure I will demand some answers,' he replied grimly.

Struggling to carry her heavy toolbox and a bulging bag of groceries, Jess let herself into her flat and stooped to pick up the post from the doormat. There were two bills, and a letter which she recognised was from the bank. For a moment her heart lurched, before she remembered that her business account was no longer in the red and she did not have to worry about paying back a hefty overdraft. Old habits died hard, she thought ruefully. She wondered if the novelty of being financially solvent would ever wear off.

On her way down the hall she glanced into Angelo's room. It was still unusually tidy—which meant that he hadn't come back. Jess frowned. It was three days since he had disappeared, and since then he hadn't answered any of her calls. Should she be worried about him? He had probably moved on to another job, like so many of the casual labourers she employed did, she told herself.

But Angelo had been different from the other labourers who asked for work. Despite his assurances that he had experience as a decorator it had quickly become apparent that he did not know one end of a paintbrush from the other. Yet he was clearly intelligent and spoke perfect English, albeit with a strong foreign accent. He had explained that he was a homeless migrant. His gentle nature reminded Jess of her best friend Daniel, whom she had known at the children's home, and perhaps that was why she had impulsively offered him the spare room in her flat until he got on his feet. Angelo had been touchingly grateful and it just wasn't like him to leave without saying goodbye—especially as he had left his stuff, including his beloved guitar, behind.

Reporting him missing seemed like an overreaction, and although it was a long time since her troubled teenage years she still had an inherent mistrust of the police. But what if he'd had an accident and was lying in hospital with no one to visit him? Jess knew too well what it was like to feel utterly alone in the world, to know that no one cared.

If she hadn't heard from him by tomorrow she would notify the police, she decided as she dumped the bag of groceries on the kitchen worktop and dug out the frozen ready meal she'd bought for dinner. She'd missed lunch. Owing to a mix-up with paint colours, the job she was working on was behind schedule—which was why Angelo's disappearance was so inconvenient. He might not be the best painter in the world—in fact he was the worst she'd ever known—but to get the contract finished on time she needed all the help she could get.

The instructions on the box of pasta Bolognese said it cooked in six minutes. Jess's stomach rumbled. Six minutes sounded like an eternity when she was starving. Taking a screwdriver from her pocket, she pierced the film lid and shoved the meal into the microwave. At least it gave her enough time for a much-needed shower. A glance in the mirror revealed that she had white emulsion in her hair from where she had been painting a ceiling.

Pulling off her boots, she headed for the bathroom, stripped off her dungarees and shirt and stepped into the shower cubicle. One day, when she could afford to buy her own flat, the first thing she would do would be to install a power shower, she thought as the ferocious jet of water washed away the dust and grime of a hard day's work. For her birthday the previous week she had treated herself to a gorgeous luxury shower *crème*. The richly perfumed lather left her skin feeling satin-soft, and using a liberal amount of shampoo she managed to rinse the paint out of her hair.

Her team of workmen would tease her unmercifully if they found out that she had a girly side, she thought ruefully. Working in an all-male environment was tough, but so was Jess—her childhood had seen to that.

The sound of the doorbell was followed almost instantly by the ping of the microwave telling her that her food was ready. Pulling on her robe as the doorbell went again, she padded barefoot back to the kitchen. Why didn't whoever was ringing the doorbell give up and go away? she wondered irritably. The microwave meal smelled unpleasantly of molten plastic, but she was too hungry to care. She peeled back the film covering and cursed as the escaping steam burnt her fingers. The doorbell rang for a third time—a long, strident peal that Jess could not ignore— and it suddenly occurred to her that maybe Angelo had come back.

Drago snatched his finger from the doorbell and uttered a curse. Clearly no one was at home. He had broken the speed limit driving from the airport to Hampstead, which was where, he had learned from his aunt's lawyer, Jess Harper lived.

According to Maurio Rochas the Englishwoman was a painter. Presumably she had a successful career to be able to afford to live in this attractive and affluent part of north-west London, Drago mused. He guessed that the Art Deco building had once been a magnificent house. It had been converted into six flats that must be highly sought after.

Maurio had not known any more information about the woman Angelo had been living with, and as yet the private investigator Drago had hired to run a check on her had not got back to him. But for now the question of why his cousin had given her money was unimportant. All that mattered was that he should persuade Jess Harper to visit Angelo. Hopefully the sound of her voice would rouse him from his unconscious state.

Where the hell *was* she? He wondered if she worked from a studio—maybe he could get the address from a neighbour. He did not have time to waste searching for her when Angelo's condition remained critical. Frustration surged through him and he pressed the doorbell again, even though he knew it was pointless. He was exhausted after spending the past three days and nights at the hospital, snatching the odd half-hour's sleep in the chair beside Angelo's bed.

His eyes felt gritty and he rubbed his hand across them as images of his cousin flashed into his mind. Angelo had been a sensitive, serious little boy after his father's death, and he had hero-worshipped Drago. It was only during the nightmare of the last few days, while Angelo hovered between life and death, that Drago had acknowledged how deeply he cared for the young man he had helped to bring up.

There was no point waiting around when it was clear that Jess Harper wasn't here, he told himself. He was about to head back down the stairs when the door of the second-floor flat suddenly opened.

'Oh!' said a voice. 'I thought you were someone else.'

Drago spun round, and as he stared at the figure standing in the doorway his breath seemed to rush from his body. He felt a strange sensation, as if his ribcage had been crushed in a vice. There had only been one other occasion in his life when he had been so blown away by a woman, and then he had been an impressionable twenty-two-year-old. Now he was thirty-seven, highly sexually experienced—and, if he was honest, somewhat jaded from a relentless diet of meaningless affairs. But for a few crazy seconds he felt like a hormone-fuelled youth again.

His nostrils flared and he gave his head a slight shake, utterly nonplussed by his reaction. He had met hundreds of beautiful women in his life, and bedded more of them than he cared to think about, but this woman quite literally took his breath away. His eyes were drawn to the front of her white towelling robe, which was gaping slightly to reveal the pale upper slopes of her breasts. The realisation that she was probably naked beneath the robe heated his blood, and every nerve-ending in his body prickled with fierce sexual awareness.

Swallowing hard, Drago studied the woman's face. It was a perfect oval, and her delicate features looked as though they had been sculpted from fine porcelain. The high cheekbones gave her an elfin quality that was further accentuated by her slanting green eyes. Her long, damp, dark red hair contrasted starkly with her pale skin.

Something unfurled deep in his gut—a primitive hunger and an inexplicable sense of possessiveness that made him want to seize her in his arms and lay claim to her.

'Can I help you?'

Her voice was soft, with a slight huskiness that made his heart jolt. He found himself hoping that his aunt's lawyer had made a mistake with the address and this woman was not his cousin's mistress. The idea of Angelo making love to her incited a feeling of violent jealousy in him.

He gave himself a mental shake, irritated by his body's unwarranted response to her, and demanded abruptly, 'Are you Jess Harper?'

Her green eyes narrowed. 'Who wants to know?'

'My name is Drago Cassari. I understand that my cousin Angelo has been living here with you.'

'Cousin!' She sounded genuinely shocked. 'Angelo told me that he was alone and had no family.'

So he had the right address, and the right woman. Drago's jaw tightened as he struggled to dismiss the image that had come into his mind of tracing the perfect cupid's-bow shape of her lips with his tongue. As he walked towards her she retreated behind the half-open door and eyed him distrustfully.

'I was unaware that Angelo had any relatives. Do you have proof that you are his cousin?'

Irritated by her suspicious tone, he withdrew his mobile phone from his jacket and accessed a photograph stored in the phone's memory.

'This is a picture of me with Angelo and his mother, taken six months ago when we attended the opening of the new Cassa di Cassari store in Milan,' he explained, handing the phone to her.

She stared at the screen for several moments. 'It's definitely Angelo, although I've never seen him wearing a tuxedo before,' she said slowly. 'But…it doesn't make sense. I don't understand why he never mentioned his family.'

Drago did not think it strange that his cousin had kept details of his private life secret. The Cassaris were one of the wealthiest families in Italy and attracted huge media attention. Drago had been hounded by the paparazzi since he was a teenager. He had learned to choose his friends carefully, and had taught his cousin to do the same. Although if the information about Jess Harper having a criminal record was true, then perhaps Angelo had not been careful enough, he mused.

The confused expression on Jess Harper's face was surprisingly convincing.

'There's a Cassa di Cassari department store in Oxford Street that sells the most beautiful but incredibly expensive bedlinen and other household furnishings.' If she ever won the lottery, Jess had promised herself that she would shop exclusively at Cassa di Cassari. 'It had never occurred to me until now that Angelo has the same name—Cassari. I suppose it's just coincidence.' She looked at the photo of the shop-opening again and her frown deepened. 'I mean—Angelo can't have any connection to a world-famous brand-name—can he?'

Could she really not know? Drago found it difficult to believe that she was unaware of Angelo's identity.

'Our great-grandfather founded Cassa di Cassari shortly after the First World War. After our fathers were killed in an accident I inherited a seventy per cent stake of the company. Angelo owns a thirty per cent share.'

Drago's eyes narrowed when Jess Harper made a startled sound. Either she really had not known the true extent of his cousin's wealth or she was a good actress. Perhaps she was wishing she had 'borrowed' more money from Angelo, he thought cynically. But for now the question of how she had got her hands on Angelo's inheritance fund wasn't important. He simply wanted to get her to Italy as quickly as possible. There would be time for questions once his cousin had regained consciousness.

She thrust his phone at him. 'I don't understand what's going on, or why Angelo lied to me, but he isn't here. He left a couple of days ago without saying where he was going and I have no idea where he is. I'm afraid I can't help you.'

She began to close the door, but with lightning reaction Drago jammed his foot in the doorway.

'He's in hospital, fighting for his life.'

Jess froze. Her anger and incomprehension that

Angelo had not been honest with her faded and she felt as if an ice cube had slithered down her spine. She was shocked to hear that he had a family and dumbstruck by the revelation that he was connected to the famous Cassa di Cassari luxury Italian homeware brand. The whole thing was unbelievable, and if it wasn't for the photo of him on Drago Cassari's phone she would have assumed it was a case of mistaken identity. But the news that Angelo was in hospital was more shocking than anything.

'Why...? I mean, is he ill?' She felt guilty that she had not reported Angelo missing. He was a nice guy, and she should have realised that he would not have moved out of her flat without saying goodbye.

'He was in a car accident. He suffered a serious head injury and has been unconscious for three days.'

Drago Cassari spoke in a controlled voice, but when Jess looked closely at him she saw lines of strain around his eyes.

She felt sick as she pictured Angelo the last time she had seen him, the evening before he had disappeared. She had cooked dinner—only omelettes, which was all her limited culinary skills could manage—and he had been flatteringly appreciative and afterwards helped with the washing up. She had been surprised to find he was gone the following morning, but she had assumed he was used to being alone, just as she was, and hadn't thought to inform her he was going away. As the days had passed she had started to worry, though—independent as he was, he was still young.

Drago Cassari's voice cut into her thoughts. 'I've come to ask if you will visit him in hospital. The longer he remains unconscious the more chance there is that he will have permanent brain damage.'

'He's that seriously hurt?' Jess swallowed as she imagined Angelo injured and unconscious. A memory flashed into her mind of seeing Daniel in Intensive Care after he had been knocked off his push-bike by a speeding car. He had looked so peaceful, as if he was asleep, but the nurse had said he was only being kept alive by the machine that was breathing for him and that he was showing no signs of brain activity. Jess had understood that Daniel was seriously injured but she hadn't expected him to die. He had only been sixteen. Even eight years later, thinking about it brought a lump to her throat.

Could Angelo die? The thought was too awful to contemplate, but from his cousin's grave expression it was clearly a possibility.

'Of course I'll visit him,' she said huskily. She had no idea why Angelo had told her he was alone and destitute, but the mystery of why he had lied wasn't important when his life was at risk.

She stared at the man who said he was Angelo's cousin and saw a faint resemblance between the two men. Both had olive skin and dark, almost black hair. But, unlike Angelo's untidy curls, Drago Cassari's hair was straight and sleek, cut short to reveal the chiselled bone structure of his features. And whilst Angelo could be described as boyishly attractive, with his soulful eyes and gentle smile, his older cousin was the most striking, *lethally* sexy man Jess had ever met.

His face was cruelly beautiful—hard and angular, with slashing cheekbones and eyes the colour of ebony beneath heavy brows. His jaw was square and his mouth unsmiling, yet the curve of his lips was innately sensual. Jess could not stop staring at his mouth—could not prevent herself from wondering what it would feel like to be kissed by him. She knew without understanding *how* she knew that his lips would be firm and he would demand total capitulation to his mastery.

Her wayward thoughts were so unexpected that she almost gasped out loud. Her gaze was drawn upwards to his eyes and she saw something flicker in their inky-dark depths that evoked a curious dragging ache deep in her pelvis. Shaken, she looked away from him and snatched a breath.

'Of course I'll come to the hospital,' she repeated. 'I'll just get some clothes on.'

As the words left her mouth she became acutely conscious that she was naked beneath her bathrobe. She stiffened as Drago Cassari subjected her to an intent scrutiny. She had the feeling that he was mentally stripping her, and she clutched the edges of the robe together, hoping he could not guess how fast her heart was beating.

The glitter in his dark eyes warned her that he was fully aware of his effect on her. She felt herself blush and wondered why she was behaving so strangely. She worked in an all-male environment and was regarded as 'one of the lads' by her team of workmen. Only once in her life had she been sexually attracted to a man, and the experience had left her with emotional scars that would never completely heal. Since then she had been too busy with her job to have time for relationships—and maybe too scared, she acknowledged honestly. She did not respond to men on a sexual level, and she was shocked by her reaction to a stranger—even if he *was* the sexiest man she had ever laid eyes on.

Drago Cassari wasn't a stranger; he was Angelo's cousin, she reminded herself. She felt ashamed for indulging in inappropriate thoughts about him when Angelo was in a critical condition. Taking a deep breath, she ignored the unsettling thought that she did not want to be alone with a man who exuded such raw sexual magnetism and pulled the door open fully to allow him to enter her flat.

'Do you want to come in and wait? It'll only take me a minute to change.'

'Thank you.' He stepped through the doorway and instantly seemed to dominate the narrow hall. He must be several inches over six feet tall, Jess estimated. The fact that he was dressed entirely in black—jeans, shirt and leather jacket—accentuated his height and powerful physique. Standing so close to him, she caught the sensual musk of his aftershave, and she felt a tingling sensation in her nipples as they hardened and rubbed against the towelling robe.

Horrified that she seemed powerless to control her reaction to him, she led the way down the hall and ushered him into the sitting room. 'If you would like to wait in here, I won't be long.'

'While you are getting ready I'll call the hospital for an update on Angelo's condition.' He glanced up from his phone. 'I hope your passport is valid.'

Halfway out of the room, Jess paused and gave him a bemused look. 'Why do I need my passport to visit a hospital? Where is Angelo, anyway? The Royal Free Hospital is the closest to here.' She hesitated. 'But I don't know where the accident happened. Was it locally?'

Drago had walked across the spacious sitting room to stand by the window. The view of the leafy suburb of Hampstead was charming. Glancing around the room, he was impressed with the excellent quality of the décor and furnishings, which reinforced his opinion that Jess Harper must have a lucrative career to be able to afford this stylish apartment.

He turned his head and it seemed to Jess his black eyes bored into her very soul. 'It happened in Italy,' he said flatly. 'On the highway between the airport and Venice. I assume Angelo was coming home, but he never made it. He's being cared for at a hospital in Mestre, which is on the mainland of Venice.'

His phone buzzed and he looked down at the screen. 'I've had a message to say that my plane has been refuelled. Can you be ready to leave for the airport in five minutes?'

CHAPTER TWO

'AIRPORT!' AS THE meaning of Drago Cassari's words slowly sank in Jess shook her head. *'I can't go to Venice!'*

In a minute she would wake up and find she'd been having a crazy dream, she thought dazedly. Maybe the six double-shot espressos she'd drunk during the day instead of eating a proper lunch were causing her to have strange hallucinations— because this could *not* be happening.

'Don't you care about Angelo? I thought you had a close relationship with him.'

Drago's harsh voice broke the silence, forcing Jess to accept that he was not a figment of her imagination.

'Of course I care that he's hurt,' she said quickly. 'But I wouldn't say that we have a close relationship, exactly. I've only known him since he started working for me about two months ago.'

'He *worked* for you?' It was Drago's turn to look puzzled. 'What kind of work? I was informed that you are a painter.' Into his mind flashed a startling image of his cousin posing for her. 'Did Angelo model for you?'

'Hardly,' Jess said drily. Crossing the room, she took a business card from the desk and handed it to him. 'I paint houses, Mr Cassari, not masterpieces.'

The card read 'T&J Decorators' and gave a phone number and a website address. Drago glanced at it and then looked back Jess, struck once again by her petite stature and fragile build. The notion that she was a manual labourer was ridiculous.

'Do you mean you are an interior designer for this decorating company? Or do you deal with office administration? I find it hard to believe that you actually paint walls for a living.'

Jess was irritated by the note of disdain she was sure she heard in his voice. 'I do some general decorating, but as a matter of fact I'm a trained chippie—a carpenter,' she explained when he frowned. 'I also act as site foreman and make sure that my workmen finish their contracts on time and follow safety procedures.'

His black brows lifted. 'It seems an unusual career choice for a woman.'

She was tempted to tell him that very few careers were available to someone who had flunked school and failed to gain any academic qualifications. She would have loved to train to be an interior designer, but most people working in the industry had an art degree, and she had more chance of flying to the moon than going to university.

'And you're saying that you employed Angelo as a decorator?' Now Drago's tone was sceptical. 'Why would he choose to work as a labourer when he belongs to one of the wealthiest families in Italy?'

'You tell me.' The situation was growing more bizarre by the minute, Jess thought. 'I took him on because I was short of staff. To be honest he was pretty hopeless at decorating, but he said he had no money and nowhere to live and I felt sorry for him. I told him he could stay with me until he could afford to rent his own place.'

Drago's expression became blatantly cynical. 'Why would you do that for someone you barely knew?'

'Because I know what it's like to reach rock-bottom.' Unbeknown to Jess her eyes darkened to deep jade as she recalled the despair she had once felt. There had been a time when she had felt she had nothing to live for—until her wonderful foster-parents had given her a home and a future.

She had sensed despair in Angelo and had wanted to help him as she had been helped by Margaret and Ted Robbins. But now she felt a fool. Why had he made up all that stuff about being poor and homeless when, according to Drago Cassari, Angelo came from a wealthy family?

She stared at Angelo's cousin, her mind reeling. 'How do you know about me?' she demanded, unsettled by his statement that he had been given information about her. It almost sounded as though he had asked someone to investigate her. The situation was so unreal that anything seemed possible.

He gave a noncommittal shrug. 'Angelo spoke about you to his mother, and obviously he gave her the address of where he was living in London.

'Oh…yes, I suppose he would have done.'

Drago studied Jess Harper speculatively for a few moments. He had no intention of revealing that he knew Angelo had given her money. He did not understand what was going on, and until he had more facts he did not want to give away too much. He checked his watch. 'We need to be going.'

'I'm sorry, but I can't go with you.' Jess bit her lip. She felt terrible about Angelo, but disappearing off to Italy simply wasn't an option. 'I have a business to run—we're behind schedule on our current contract and I can't—'

'He spoke your name.' Drago cut her off in a driven voice. His accent was suddenly very pronounced, as if he was struggling to control his emotions. 'This morning Angelo roused very briefly and he asked for you.'

He walked towards her, his midnight-dark eyes never leaving her face. 'You might be his best hope of recovery. Hearing your voice might be the key that will release him from his prison and bring him back to his family.'

Jess swallowed. 'Mr Cassari…'

'Drago,' he said huskily. 'You are Angelo's friend, so I think we should dispense with formalities.'

He halted in front of her and Jess had to tilt her head to look up at his face. She felt overwhelmed by his height and sheer physical presence. Her heart slammed against her ribs when he laid a finger lightly across her lips to prevent her from speaking.

'*Please*, Jess. Angelo needs you. *I* need you to come with me. I think of him as my brother, even my son—for since his father died I have tried to be a father to him.'

Dear heaven, how could she refuse such a heartfelt entreaty? The raw emotion in Drago's voice made Jess's heart ache. Only a few days ago she had listened to Angelo playing his guitar, but now he was fighting for his life. She thought of Daniel, who had never regained consciousness. Surely if there was a chance she could help Angelo she must try?

Her common sense argued that she would be crazy to agree to go away with a man she had never met before, but she was haunted by the image of Daniel the last time she had seen him. He had died a few hours after her visit. She hadn't been allowed to attend his funeral—the head of the care home had decided it would be too upsetting—and so she had never had a chance to say goodbye.

'All right,' she said shakily. 'I'll come. But I need to make some phone calls and arrange for someone to cover for me at work.'

Mike could take over as foreman while she was away. She trusted him, and knew he would push her team of decorators to get the contract finished. Thoughts raced through Jess's head. She was fiercely proud of T&J Decorators and hated the thought of leaving it even for a few days. Like most businesses in the construction industry, the company had suffered because of the economic recession, but thankfully the windfall of money she had recently received meant that T&J was now financially stable—as long as she kept working hard and securing new contracts.

'I can only be away for a couple of days,' she warned.

She glanced at Drago and felt a tiny flicker of unease when she found him watching her intently. He was so big and imposing, and there was a faintly predatory expression in his eyes that made her think of a lethal jungle cat preparing to make a kill—and she was the prey. But when she blinked and refocused on him she cursed herself for being over-imaginative. His smile was dangerously attractive but the only thing she had to worry about was her unexpected reaction to him.

'Thank you,' he murmured in the husky accent that sent a shiver across her skin. 'I hope that Angelo will respond when he hears your voice. When it is time for you to leave Italy I will arrange for you be flown home on my plane.'

Once the matter of Angelo's missing inheritance fund had been resolved, Drago thought to himself. As Jess stepped away from him his eyes were drawn to the deep vee of her robe, which revealed the curve of her breasts, and he felt a sharp stab of desire in his gut as he imagined untying the belt around her slender waist and sliding his hand inside the towelling folds. The glimpse of her body evoked a picture in his mind of her lying beneath him, her milky-pale thighs entwined with his darker olive-toned limbs. Light and dark, soft and hard, fiery Latin male and cool English rose.

He met her startled gaze and was intrigued to see soft colour stain her cheeks. The mysterious alchemy of sexual attraction was impossible to explain, he mused. He recognised that she felt it as fiercely as he did, and under different circumstances he would have wasted no time in bedding her. But the circumstances could not be more wrong. His cousin was critically injured and, for all her apparent concern for Angelo, Jess Harper had a lot of explaining to do. For now, Drago was prepared to keep an open mind, but he could not risk his judgement being undermined by indulging in fantasies of her naked in his arms.

The sound of her voice dragged him from his uncomfortable thoughts. 'I'll get dressed, and if you don't mind quickly have my dinner,' she said as she hurried over to the door. 'I haven't eaten all day. It was ready when you arrived and it will only take a couple of seconds to reheat.'

'*Santa Madonna!* You mean that terrible smell is your evening meal?' Drago was genuinely horrified. 'I thought you had problems with the drains.'

Jess felt a spurt of annoyance at his arrogant tone. There had been plenty of times in the past when she hadn't been able to afford to buy even the cheapest supermarket budget food, and even though she now had money she was careful with it. She doubted Drago Cassari had ever known what it felt like to be so hungry that you felt sick, or so cold that your bones ached, as she had often been as a child.

'I take it you don't often dine on microwave meals?' she said drily.

His eyes narrowed at her sarcastic tone. 'Nor do I ever intend to. There's no time for you to eat now. We'll have dinner on the plane. Please hurry,' he added impatiently. 'While you are wasting time Angelo's condition may be worsening.'

By the time they landed at Marco Polo airport Jess was under no illusion about what kind of man Drago Cassari was. Powerful, compelling and utterly self-assured, he took control of every situation with quiet authority, and she'd noticed that everyone around him, from the airport staff to the crew on his private jet, treated him with a deference few men could command.

Maybe it was his wealth that set him apart from ordinary people and gave him an air of suave sophistication. She guessed he must be well-off. Let's face it, how many people had she ever met who owned their own plane? she thought wryly. When they had boarded his jet a uniformed steward had ushered her over to one of the opulent leather sofas in the cabin and offered her a glass of champagne. During the flight the dinner they had been served had been exquisite—the sort of food she imagined you would expect at a five-star restaurant. She felt as though she had entered a different world where she had no place, but in which Drago was completely at home.

Now, as they walked through the airport foyer, she was conscious that her jeans were scruffy and her tee shirt, which had shrunk in the wash, revealed a strip of bare midriff when she moved.

In contrast, Drago looked as if he had stepped from the pages of a glossy magazine, with his designer clothes and stunning good looks. The shadow of dark stubble on his jaw added to his potent sex appeal, and as he strode slightly ahead of her Jess noticed the interested glances he attracted from virtually every female he passed.

He was talking into his phone, which had been clamped to his ear for most of the flight from England, and although he spoke in Italian she guessed from his lowered brows that he was not happy. A cold hand of fear gripped her heart as she wondered if Angelo's condition was worse. *Please, God, don't let him die*, she offered up in silent prayer. Twenty-two was too young for anyone to leave this world—especially someone as sweet and gentle as Angelo. They had become good friends while they had been flatmates. But she was still reeling from the discovery that he came from a wealthy family and was related to this formidable man who had now halted in front of the airport doors and was waiting for her to catch up with him.

'Were you talking to someone at the hospital? Has something happened with Angelo?' she asked anxiously.

'There's no change,' Drago replied curtly.

He wondered if the concern in Jess's voice was genuine or whether she was simply adept at fooling people. During the flight he had tried to think about her objectively, bearing in mind that all he knew about her so far was that she had a criminal record and had either begged, borrowed or stolen a fortune from his cousin. But to his intense irritation he had been distracted by his physical reaction to her, and had found himself admiring her hair—which, now that it had dried, reminded him of the colour of autumn leaves: a glorious mixture of red, copper and gold, which rippled down her back and shimmered like raw silk.

He noted how her fashionable skinny jeans emphasised her slender figure and her long-sleeved tee shirt clung to her small breasts. With a rucksack over one shoulder and a guitar hanging from the other she looked as if she was going to a pop festival rather than to visit a hospital. Her clothes were totally inappropriate, he thought irritably, and he was certain she wasn't wearing a bra—

although her breasts were pert enough that she did not need to.

Trying to ignore the flare of heat in his groin, he said, 'I've just heard from the head of my security team that the press have got wind of the accident. Probably one of the hospital staff tipped them off,' he growled angrily. 'The paparazzi are hanging around the hospital, and they must have heard that my plane just landed because there's a mob of reporters waiting outside the airport. Stick close to me. I'll make sure no one hassles you,' he reassured her when he saw her startled expression. 'My car is on its way to pick us up, and Fico, my bodyguard, will clear a path for us.'

'You have a bodyguard?' she said faintly.

He shrugged, drawing Jess's attention to his broad shoulders and a muscular physique that indicated he followed a punishing workout regime.

'I can take care of myself, but it's sensible to take precautions. I am well-known in Italy, and there have been a couple of kidnap attempts in the past. Many criminal gangs would love to get hold of me and demand a billion-pound ransom,' he told her.

He did not seem unduly worried, and looked amused when she could not disguise her shock at his revelation that he was a billionaire.

'It's amazing what some people will do for money,' he murmured sardonically.

It was dark outside, but through the glass doors Jess could see a large crowd of shadowy figures moving around. 'Let me take your bag,' Drago ordered, lifting her rucksack from her shoulders. He looked surprised when he felt how light it was. 'There can't be much in here. I told you to bring clothes for a few days, in case Angelo doesn't immediately respond to your voice.'

It was only natural that he was concerned for his cousin, but *jeez*, he was bossy! Jess lifted her chin. 'I've brought everything I own that isn't covered in paint. I don't have many clothes.'

'Or any that fit properly, seemingly,' he drawled as he raked his eyes over her too-small tee shirt and lingered on her breasts.

To her horror Jess felt her nipples harden, and knew they must be clearly visible beneath her clingy top. She wished she had made a better search for one of the few bras she possessed, which had inconveniently disappeared from her underwear drawer. She rarely wore a bra because she felt more comfortable working without one, but she had not bargained on her body's embarrassing reaction to Drago. Against her will her gaze was drawn to his, and her heart jolted against her ribs when she saw the unmistakable glint of sexual awareness in his black eyes.

This could not be happening, she thought dazedly. A few hours ago it had just been an ordinary day—until a darkly handsome stranger had turned up at her flat. Now she had been whisked to Italy on a private jet to visit Angelo, who was not the penniless migrant he had led her to believe but a member of the hugely wealthy Cassari family. Even more disturbing was the way she reacted to Angelo's cousin. She hated how her body responded to Drago's virile masculinity. Not since she had dated Sebastian Loxley had she felt so unsettled by a man. The memory of her one brief love affair—although it could hardly be called that, because Seb had never loved her— served as a stark reminder of why she needed to ignore her dangerous attraction to Drago.

He was watching her from beneath hooded eyelids that hid his expression, so that she had no idea what he was thinking. Just then the door behind him opened, and as he turned his attention to the thickset man who appeared Jess released her breath on a shaky sigh.

The man spoke to Drago in rapid Italian. He replied in the same language and then glanced back at Jess. 'The car is outside. Let's get this over with,' he growled.

To Jess's shock he gripped her arm and pulled her close to his side. She was intensely conscious of his hard body pressed against hers, and the sensual musk of his aftershave swamped her senses. But then he opened the door and she was blinded by an explosion of bright flashing lights.

Despite the efforts of the bodyguard the reporters closed in on them like a pack of wolves, and a cacophony of voices shouting words she did not understand bombarded her ears. It seemed like a lifetime until they reached the black limousine waiting with its engine already running.

Drago pulled open the car door. 'Get in and we'll soon be away from this madness.' He swore when he saw her struggling to climb inside with the guitar still strapped to her back. '*Madonna!* Was it necessary to bring this with you?' he muttered as he tugged the strap over her shoulder. He pushed her into the seat and thrust the guitar onto her lap before sliding into the car after her. 'Are you expecting Angelo to wake at the sound of your strumming? I think you must have watched too many romantic films.'

'Hearing music might rouse him,' Jess snapped, infuriated by his sarcasm. 'The guitar isn't mine; it's Angelo's. I thought he would like to have it with him when he regains consciousness. You *must* know how much his guitar means to him?'

'I didn't know he could play an instrument,' Drago said bluntly.

'But he plays all the time, and he's a brilliant guitarist. He told me his dream is to play professionally.' She stared at him. 'How come you know so little about your cousin? You say you think of him as a brother, but you don't seem to know the first thing about him.'

Drago was annoyed by the implied criticism

in her voice. 'Just because I was unaware of his hobby does not mean I'm not close to him.'

Jess shook her head. 'It's not just a hobby. Music is Angelo's passion.'

The limousine was now streaking along the highway, but the sound of the engine was barely discernible inside the car. The privacy glass separated them from the driver and bodyguard who were sitting in the front, and enclosed them in the rear in a dark, silent space that was shattered by Jess's fervent outburst. She tensed when Drago turned his head and subjected her to a slow appraisal.

'Passion?' he murmured, in the deep, accented voice that caressed her senses like rough velvet.

The word seemed to hover in the air between them. Jess's mouth felt dry and she wet her lips with the tip of her tongue as a shocking image flashed into her mind of Drago pushing her back against the leather seat and covering her mouth with his. It was utterly crazy, but she longed for him to kiss her with the heated passion she sensed burned within him. She pictured him running his hands over her body and sliding them beneath her tee shirt to caress her breasts and stroke her nipples that were as hard as pebbles from her erotic thoughts.

She shuddered, acutely conscious of the flood of heat between her legs. Dear heaven, what was happening to her? Even worse, he *knew* the effect he was having on her. The unnerving predatory expression that she had told herself she had imagined back at her flat had returned to his eyes, and she could almost taste the sexual tension simmering in the air between them.

Drago shrugged. 'I admit I did not know of Angelo's interest in music. What about you—are you a musician too?'

'No. Angelo taught me to play a couple of tunes on the guitar, but I'm not very good.'

He trapped her gaze and his voice took on a husky quality that caused the tiny hairs on Jess's body to stand on end.

'So—what is *your* passion, Jess?'

She swallowed, and searched her mind desperately for something to say—some way to break the spell he seemed to have cast on her. 'I…I make things from wood…sculptures and ornate

carvings. I suppose you could say that is my passion. I love the feel of wood—its smoothness and
the fact that it feels alive when I shape it. It's very
tactile, and I love creating sculptures that invite
people to touch them, stroke their polished sur-
faces—'

She broke off abruptly, embarrassed by her enthusiasm. Drago could not possibly understand
how she poured all the painful emotions that
were locked up inside her into her sculptures.
Of all the wonderful things that Ted, her fos-
ter-father, had done for her, teaching her how to
work with wood meant the most to her, because
he had given her a way to express herself and
unlocked an artistic talent that had given her a
sense of self-worth.

She was relieved when Drago's phone rang.
While he took the call she stared out of the window and watched the street lamps flash past in
a blur as the car sped along the highway. A few
minutes later the imposing modern building of
the Venice-Mestre Hospital came into view. As
they approached Jess saw dozens more reporters crowded around the entrance, and when the

limousine halted outside the front doors camera flashbulbs lit up the interior of the car, throwing Drago's stern features into sharp relief.

'Do the press always hound you like this?' she asked him. She felt nervous about leaving the car, even with the reassuring presence of his huge bodyguard.

'The paparazzi often follow me—they have a relentless fascination with my love-life,' he said drily. 'But I will not allow them to upset my aunt and mother. I'll issue a statement about Angelo's accident in the morning and ask for my family to be given privacy while his condition remains critical. Hopefully that will make a few of them back off.'

When the driver opened the door Drago climbed out of the car first and turned to offer Jess his hand. The sound of loud, unintelligible voices hit her ears, and she instinctively ducked her head to avoid the flashlights. The crowd of reporters pushed forward and she stumbled—would have fallen but for the arm that Drago snaked around her waist. Half carrying her, he hurried her through the main doors of the hospital while the reporters were prevented from entering by several security guards.

'Are you all right?' he asked, glancing at her tense face.

'Yes, I'm fine.' No way was Jess going to admit that being in close proximity to his hard body had made her heart race. As she followed Drago along a corridor her heart began to pound for a different reason. She hated hospitals—hated the frightening clinical atmosphere and the smell of disinfectant that were such a painful reminder not only of Daniel, but of her own brief stay on a hospital ward when she was seventeen.

A nurse met them at the door of the intensive care ward, and while Drago spoke to her Jess struggled against a rising sense of panic. All her life she had learned to block out unhappy experiences—and there had been plenty of those during her childhood, both before and after she had gone into care—but being in the hospital brought back agonising memories that she had never been able to bury. She did not want to think about Daniel. And she did not dare think about

Katie. Opening that particular Pandora's box was simply too painful.

Her instincts screamed at her to turn and run from the ward. But it was too late. Drago had halted and was opening a door which she saw led into a small private room. She glimpsed a figure lying on a bed surrounded by machinery which beeped and flashed sporadically.

'Maybe we shouldn't disturb Angelo now,' she said shakily. 'It's nearly midnight. Do the staff mind us being here outside of visiting hours?'

'Of course not.' Drago's dark brows rose in surprise. 'We can come whenever we want. Until this morning when I flew to London I hadn't left the ward since Angelo was admitted. As for disturbing him—that is the point of bringing you here,' he said sardonically. He glanced at her and frowned when he saw that her face was so white that the golden freckles on her nose and cheeks stood out. 'Did the reporters upset you? Why are you so pale?'

Jess fought the nauseous sensation that swept over her. 'I don't like hospitals,' she muttered.

'Does anyone?' Impatience crept into Drago's voice. His jaw tightened.

The past days he had spent at the hospital had evoked painful memories that would always haunt him. It had been a long time ago, he reminded himself. Life had moved on. He was thankful that Vittoria had found happiness with the man she had eventually married, and now she had a child. God knew she deserved to be happy after everything that had happened, the way he had let her down…

With an effort he forced his mind from the past and concentrated on the woman at his side. 'I can assure you that my aunt would rather not be here, keeping a vigil at her son's bedside.' He hesitated and deliberately lowered his voice so that only Jess could hear him. 'Angelo's mother is understandably distraught. You must forgive her if she is a little…abrupt.'

Jess did not understand what Drago meant, but there was no time to query his curious statement as he ushered her into the room. As she nervously approached the bed a horrible sense of dread and déjà-vu filled her. Angelo looked very different without his wild curls half-hiding his face. His skull was covered in bandages and his skin and lips were deathly pale. He reminded her of a wax-work figure: perfect in detail but lifeless, just as Daniel had been.

Hot tears suddenly burned her eyes. She rarely cried; experience had taught her that it was a pointless exercise. But for once she could not control her emotions. It seemed so cruel that a young man in the prime of his life might never open his eyes again or smile at the people he loved.

A movement from the other side of the room made Jess turn her head, and she saw a woman whom she guessed from her strained face and red-rimmed eyes to be Angelo's mother.

Overwhelmed by an instinctive need to express her sympathy, Jess murmured, 'I'm so sorry about Angelo.'

The woman stared at her, and then spoke to Drago in a torrent of Italian. Jess could not understand a word, but she sensed that her presence was not welcome. Remembering Drago's warning that his aunt was distraught, she wondered if she should leave and come back to visit Angelo later, but as she turned towards the door Drago placed a firm hand on her shoulder and pushed her forward.

'Aunt Dorotea, Jess has come to talk to Angelo in the hope that he will respond to her voice.' He looked steadily at his aunt. 'I'm sure you appreciate that she has rushed from England to visit him.'

His aunt continued to stare at Jess, with no hint of welcome on her rather haughty face. But then she said sharply, 'You are my son's girlfriend?'

'I am his *friend*,' Jess corrected her.

'So you are not his mistress?'

'No.' Jess frowned, puzzled by Angelo's mother's distinctly unfriendly attitude. She glanced questioningly at Drago. 'I could come back another time, if you think it would be better.'

He shook his head. 'I brought you here to talk to Angelo. Your name is the only word he has uttered, so perhaps he will respond to you.' He looked at his aunt. 'I want you to go home for a few hours. Fico is waiting to take you. You need to get some rest and have something to eat. You will not be any help to Angelo if you collapse,' he added, countering his aunt's attempt to argue.

Despite her obvious reluctance to leave her son, his Aunt Dorotea nodded as if she was used to her nephew taking charge. 'You will call me if there is any change?'

Drago's voice softened. 'Of course.'

He escorted his aunt from the room, leaving Jess alone with Angelo. She sat by the bed, watching him, just as she had done with Daniel when one of the care workers from the home had taken her to visit him. Angelo looked so young and defenceless. It was agonising to think that he might not survive. Her throat ached, but she swallowed her tears and leaned closer to take hold of his hand. It felt warm, and that filled her with hope.

'Hi, Angelo...' she said huskily. 'What have you done to yourself?' It was difficult to know what to say, but after a moment's hesitation she continued, 'The guys missed you when you didn't show up for work. Gaz said you make the best tea. We've nearly finished the Connaught Road job. I've just got to fit new skirting boards.'

She felt comfortable talking about work and kept up a flow of chatter, although her heart sank when Angelo did not make any kind of response.

A slight sound from behind her alerted her to the fact that Drago had come back to the room and was leaning against the wall, his arms crossed over his broad chest. Immediately Jess felt self-conscious. 'My coming here hasn't done any good,' she told him flatly. 'He hasn't shown the slightest flicker of reaction.'

'We can't expect a miracle. All we can do is keep trying.' Drago walked over to the bed and stared at his cousin's motionless form. He knew it was stupid to feel disappointed that Angelo had shown no sign he had heard Jess. He had put too much faith in her. But, *Dio*, he was desperate—and he *had* hoped for a miracle, he acknowledged heavily.

'I overheard some of what you were saying to him,' he said abruptly. 'I admit I still find it hard to imagine that are you a decorator. You don't look the type to do manual work.'

She shrugged. 'I'm stronger than I look.'

Studying her slender figure, Drago was tempted

to disagree. She seemed more upset by seeing Angelo than he had expected. Her delicate features looked almost pinched, and earlier he had watched her blinking back tears. Her eyes looked huge in her pale face and there was a vulnerability about her that was unexpected.

If it wasn't for the phone call he had received a few minutes ago from the private investigator he might have been taken in by her. But the confirmation that she *was* a petty crook who had been found guilty of fraud a few years ago increased his suspicion that she had used some underhand and possibly illegal means to get her grubby hands on his cousin's inheritance fund. If necessary he was prepared to use equally underhanded methods to get the money back, Drago thought grimly.

CHAPTER THREE

JESS DRAGGED HER eyes from Drago, wishing she did not find him so unnerving. He had removed his leather jacket and she could not help noticing how his black silk shirt moulded his broad chest and clung to the ridges of his abdominal muscles. The contrast between his strong, powerful body and his cousin's unconscious form emphasised the seriousness of Angelo's condition.

She leaned closer to the bed and touched Angelo's hand, which lay limply on top of the sheet. 'I'll carry on talking and perhaps I'll get through to him.'

'I think it's unlikely anything will happen tonight,' Drago said roughly.

He could not explain the fierce objection he felt to the sight of Jess holding his cousin's hand. She had denied that they were lovers, but who knew what methods she had used to persuade Angelo to give her his inheritance fund? He had brought her to the hospital in the hope that Angelo would respond to her voice, but after hearing the information the private investigator had dug up about her he was impatient to demand some answers.

He glanced at his watch and saw that it was past midnight. He could not remember the last time he had slept and his brain ached.

'I've arranged for a nurse to sit with Angelo for the rest of the night. You will come home with me, so that you can sleep, and we'll return in the morning and try talking to him again.'

Jess stiffened. She disliked being in a hospital, with all the memories it evoked, but it was preferable to accompanying Drago to his home. The prospect of being alone with him made her heart lurch—although he might have a family, her mind pointed out.

'Are you married?' she asked abruptly. The speculative look he gave her made her feel uncomfortable, and she flushed.

'No. Why do you ask?'

'I just thought it wouldn't be fair to disturb your wife—and children if you have any.'

'Well, I don't.' His voice was suddenly terse.

'Even so, I don't mind staying here. I'll sleep in the chair if I need to. Or I could find a hotel. There must be a hotel near to the hospital.' Hopefully a budget one that wasn't too expensive, Jess thought to herself.

Drago shook his head. 'I have already asked my housekeeper to prepare a room for you.' Seeing that she wanted to continue the argument, he said in a softer tone, 'You are not going to reject my hospitality, are you, Jess? Having rushed you to Italy, the least I can do is offer you somewhere comfortable to stay.'

This was a man used to having his own way, Jess realised. Behind his persuasive smile and his sexy voice that brought her skin out in goosebumps she sensed an iron will. But in truth she was so tired that she could barely think straight. She had got up at six that morning—yesterday morning—she amended when she glanced at the clock on the wall and saw that she had been up for nearly nineteen hours. The idea of walking around a strange town looking for a hotel did not appeal.

'All right,' she murmured. 'I'll stay at your house for the rest of the night. Thank you.'

'Good.' Drago felt a spurt of satisfaction. Until he knew the truth about Jess Harper he wanted to know her whereabouts every second of the day and night, and while she was staying at his home she would be in his control.

They left the hospital by a back door to avoid the reporters still congregated at the main entrance. Jess leaned back against the seat and closed her eyes as the car sped away. Reaction to the events of the past few hours was setting in, and part of her still wondered if she was going to wake up and find her life was back to normal.

She must have dozed and woke with a start at the sound of Drago's voice.

'Wake up. We've crossed the bridge and we're about to swap the car for a boat.'

She was startled. Her lashes flew upwards and she saw that they had arrived at a marina.

'There are no roads on the islands that make up the historical city of Venice,' Drago explained as he led the way along a jetty and jumped aboard a motorboat.

Jess viewed the gap between the jetty and the boat nervously, having no wish to miss her footing and fall into the water. But as she hesitated Drago clamped his hands around her waist and lifted her down onto the deck. The brief contact with his body sent a tremor through her, but she assured herself that she was simply reacting to the cool night air after the stifling warmth of the car.

He must have noticed her shiver, because he pulled off his jacket and handed it to her, saying roughly, 'Here—put this round you.'

Not wanting to appear ungrateful, she draped the jacket over her shoulders. The leather was as soft as butter, and the silk lining still retained the heat from his body and the scent of his aftershave. Oh, *hell*, Jess thought ruefully, feeling her heart rate accelerate in response to his potent masculinity. He started the boat's engine and as they moved away from the jetty her sense of apprehension grew. It had been a mistake to come to Italy with Drago, and an even greater mistake to have allowed him to talk her into agreeing to stay at his home, but bar diving over the side and swimming back to shore she had no choice but to go with him.

Her thoughts were distracted by the breathtaking sight of Venice in the moonlight. The Grand Canal wound through the city like a long black ribbon dappled with silver moonbeams, while the water at its edges reflected the golden lights streaming from the windows of the houses that lined the two banks.

'What a beautiful building,' Jess murmured as the boat drew steadily towards a vast, elegant house which had four tiers of arched windows and several balconies. 'It looks like a medieval palace.'

'That's exactly what it is. It was built in the early fifteenth century by one of my ancestors and has belonged to the Cassari family since then.'

'You're kidding—right?' Her smile faded when she realised Drago was serious.

'The name Palazzo d'Inverno means Winter Palace—so named because traditionally the family lived here during the winter and spring, but spent the hot summer months at a house in the

Italian Alps.' Drago steered the boat alongside a wooden jetty and looped a rope around a bollard before jumping out. 'Give me your hand,' he ordered.

It was a fair leap onto the jetty so Jess reluctantly obeyed, feeling a tingling sensation like an electrical shock shoot up her arm when his fingers closed around hers.

'Does Angelo live here?' she asked, staring up at the magnificent house rather than meet Drago's far too knowing gaze.

'He has an apartment in one of the wings, and my mother and aunt have accommodation in another wing.'

Jess fell silent as she followed Drago along the stone walkway that ran beside this part of the canal. He led her up a flight of steps and through a huge, ornately carved front door. 'I told the staff not to wait up,' he explained as he ushered her into the quiet house. 'They are all fond of Angelo and the past few days have been a strain for everyone.'

The entrance hall was vast, and their footsteps rang on the marble floor and on the sweeping staircase that wound up through the centre of the house.

'This is your room,' Drago announced at last, stopping at the far end of a long corridor. He opened the door and Jess could not restrain a startled gasp as she walked past him. The proportions of the room were breathtaking, and as she lifted her eyes to the ceiling high above she was amazed to see that it had been decorated with a series of frescoes depicting plump cherubs and figures that she guessed were characters from Roman mythology.

'Thank heavens I don't work as a decorator in Venice,' she murmured. 'How on earth did anyone get up there to paint such exquisite artwork?'

The bed was covered in a cobalt blue satin bedspread, and the floor-length curtains were made of the same rich material. Walking across the plush cream velvet carpet to the window, she stared down at the canal below and watched a gondola decorated with lanterns glide past.

'I don't understand why Angelo let me think he had no money or family,' she said flatly. 'Was it some kind of joke to him?' She felt angry and hurt that Angelo had played her for a fool, but she was more furious that she had allowed herself to be duped. God, if she had learned anything from Seb surely it was never to trust anyone.

'It doesn't make sense to me, either.'

Alerted by a curious nuance in Drago's tone, Jess spun round and found that he had come up silently behind her. Once again she was struck by his height and muscular physique, and as she lifted her eyes to his face she felt a flicker of unease at his grim expression.

'I can think of no possible reason why he would have made up a story that he was destitute,' he said in a hard voice. 'My cousin is inherently honest. But I suspect that *you* are a liar, Jess Harper.'

'Excuse me?' She wondered if she had heard him correctly. At the hospital, when he had persuaded her to stay at his house, he had exerted an easy charm, but there was no hint of friendliness now in eyes that were as hard as shards of obsidian. 'I'm not a liar,' she said angrily.

'In that case I assume you will tell me the truth about why you persuaded my cousin to give you a million pounds?'

Jess's jaw dropped. 'Angelo never gave me anything,' she stammered. 'In London he didn't have a penny, and if I hadn't paid for his food he would have starved.' She pushed her hair back from her face with a trembling hand, feeling that she was sinking ever deeper into a nightmare. 'This is crazy. I don't understand anything. Why do you think Angelo gave me money—let alone such an incredible amount?'

'Because he told his mother he had done so,' Drago said coolly. 'My aunt was concerned when she learned from Angelo's financial adviser that he had withdrawn his entire inheritance fund from the bank. She asked him what he had done with the money and he said he had given it to you.'

Jess drew a sharp breath. 'But he *didn't*, I swear. I know nothing about any money.'

Drago's eyes narrowed. He had expected her to deny it, but he was surprised by how convincing she sounded. Did he want to believe her because he was intrigued by her fey beauty? taunted a voice inside his head.

Dismissing the unwelcome thought, he said

harshly, 'I think you do. I also think you were fully aware of Angelo's identity. I admit the situation is not clear to me yet, but I'm convinced that you somehow conned him into giving you a fortune. I don't know how you did it, but I intend to find out—and I warn you that I will use every means available to me to make sure you repay the money.'

'This is outrageous,' Jess snapped, anger rapidly replacing her disbelief at Drago's shocking accusation. 'I don't have to listen to this…this fantasy story you've concocted.' She swung away from him and hurried over to the door, but his next words halted her in her tracks.

'It's not a fantasy that you were convicted of fraud a few years ago, is it?'

Shock ricocheted through Jess and the blood drained from her face. She did not hear Drago's footsteps on the thick carpet, and she flinched when he caught hold of her arm and jerked her round to face him.

'The private investigator I hired to look into your background found evidence of your criminal record, so don't waste your time denying it.'

She shivered at the coldness in his black eyes. 'It wasn't what it seems,' she muttered.

He ignored her and continued ruthlessly, 'You were found guilty. It was only because you were seventeen at the time you committed the offence that you were ordered to carry out community service rather than receive a custodial sentence.'

Shame swept through Jess, even though she had nothing to feel ashamed of. The fraud charge had been a mistake, but no one had believed her. The evidence had been stacked against her—Seb had made sure of it, she thought bitterly. She had been found guilty of a crime she had unwittingly committed, set up by the man she had loved and who had told her he loved her.

The arrogant expression on Drago's face made her wish she could crawl away and hide. She cringed when she recalled how she'd thought she had sensed a sexual chemistry between them. Now she knew that he had been watching her so closely because he believed she was a common criminal, not because he was attracted to her.

'I know nothing about Angelo's missing money,'

she insisted. 'It isn't fair to accuse me just because of something that happened years ago.'

To her surprise, Drago nodded. 'You're right—it's not up to me to find out the truth. That's the job of the police. And I am sure that when I hand you over to them tomorrow they will quickly establish whether you are innocent or guilty.' His brows rose at the sound of her swiftly indrawn breath. 'Now, why does the mention of the police cause you to look so worried, I wonder?' he drawled.

'It doesn't,' Jess lied.

She had nothing to hide, but the memory of when she had been arrested and the claustrophobic terror she had felt when she had been locked in a police cell made her tremble. On the rough estate where she had spent her early childhood the police had been mistrusted by many people, including her father, and she had grown up with an intrinsic wariness of authority.

Drago strolled over to the door. 'Well, you've got a few hours to come up with an explanation about Angelo's missing inheritance fund. *Buonanotte*, Jess. I'd try to get some sleep if I were you. You're going to need your wits about you tomorrow.'

Jess stared at the door as he closed it behind him, feeling another jolt of shock when she heard a key turn in the lock. *'Hey!'* Disbelief turned to anger as she tried the handle and found that it wouldn't move. She hammered on the solid oak. 'Let me out of here. You have no right to imprison me.'

'My cousin's missing a million pounds gives me every right' came the curt reply. 'By the way, you can make as much noise as you like—no one will hear you. My room is at the other end of the hall, and the staff quarters are on the other side of the house.'

If this was a crazy dream it would be helpful if she could wake up now, before she attempted her daring escape plan, Jess thought some twenty minutes later. But as she stood on the balcony outside her room the whisper of the cool night breeze on her face and the faint lapping sound of the water in the canal were very real. It was fortunate that her room was on the second storey of the house rather than the top floor, but the canal path below still looked a long way down and she almost lost her nerve.

But the prospect of being questioned by the police and having to try to convince them that she knew nothing about Angelo's missing money filled her with dread. Drago clearly thought she had conned his cousin out of his inheritance fund, and because of her criminal record the police were likely to share his suspicions. The only person who could clear her name was Angelo, but until he regained consciousness she once again stood accused of something she had not done.

The image of Drago's haughty expression flashed into her mind. How *dared* he imprison her in his house? Her spurt of temper steadied her nerves, and after checking that the sheets she had stripped from the bed and knotted together were tied securely to the balcony she climbed over the balustrade and began to inch down the makeshift rope. Thankfully it took her weight.

It was lucky she was so agile and had a head for heights. In her job she was used to climbing up and down scaffolding, but when she looked down and saw how far away the ground was she felt sick with terror. Deciding not to glance down again, she continued her cautious journey, buoyed by the thought that Drago Cassari was in for one hell of a surprise in the morning.

'Leaving us so soon, Miss Harper?' a familiar voice enquired smoothly.

Giving a startled cry, Jess lost her grip and fell. She closed her eyes, waiting to feel the impact of her body hitting the stone path, but instead two hands roughly grabbed hold of her and her fall was cushioned by Drago's broad chest.

'*Santa Madonna!* You crazy fool,' he growled as he set her on her feet, fury blazing in his eyes as she swayed unsteadily.

Jess was so shocked she could not speak, but Drago had no problem voicing his feelings.

'You could have been killed.' He glanced up at the balcony above them and shuddered. 'I can only assume you *do* know more than you've admitted about Angelo's missing money as you were prepared to risk your life trying to get away from me.'

'I refuse to be held against my will by an *am-*

ateur sleuth who has made a totally unfounded accusation against me,' Jess snapped.

Now that she was safely on the ground she could see how dangerous her escape attempt had been, and she felt sick when she imagined how badly injured she might have been if she had fallen. But it was Drago's fault that she had been forced to take such a risk. Her temper sizzled.

'I came to Italy because I wanted to try to help Angelo, but if you think I'm going to stick around and take your accusations and insults you'd better think again,' she said hotly. 'Instead of hounding me you should be asking yourself why your cousin seemed so worried and unhappy while he was in London. I could tell that something was troubling him, but he didn't confide in me—or in you, apparently. So much for your assertion that you think of him as your brother—it seems to me that you didn't think about him enough, because if you had you would have known that something was wrong.'

Drago's face darkened. 'You know nothing about my relationship with my cousin,' he growled.

He was infuriated by her criticism, but part of his anger was fuelled by guilt that there was some truth in what Jess said. He had been so busy running Cassa di Cassari, and he had assumed that Angelo was doing well at college in London. It had been a relief to relinquish some of the responsibility he felt for his family, and although his aunt had been upset that Angelo hardly ever phoned home Drago had felt glad that his cousin was becoming independent. He'd had no idea that the young man had been unhappy—but he only had Jess's word on his cousin's state of mind, he thought grimly. And he didn't have any faith in the word of a woman who had been convicted of fraud.

'Where do you think you're going?' he demanded when she jerked away from him and swung her rucksack onto her back.

'Home.' Shaking back her glorious Titian hair, she flashed him a glittering glance from her green eyes. 'I've decided to forgo the pleasure of your hospitality,' she said with heavy irony. 'Just point me in the direction of the nearest airport and I'll be on my way.'

'The hell you will. You said you would stay until Angelo regained consciousness,' Drago reminded her.

'That was before I realised what an arrogant bully you are.'

Jess's voice rose, drawing the attention of a group of people who were walking across a nearby bridge over the canal. They were Americans, Drago realised when he overheard one of them speak in a distinctive accent. Many of the thousands of tourists who visited Venice each year preferred to come in the spring, to avoid the heat and the crowds who packed St Mark's Square in the summer months.

He saw Jess glance at the people, and caught the flash of relief on her face as she realised they spoke English. It was easy to read her mind. She had proved when she had climbed down from the balcony that she was surprisingly resourceful and determined. There was only one way Drago could think of to stop her from creating a scene, and before she had time to comprehend his intention he pulled her into his arms and lowered his head, muffling her startled cry with his lips.

As he had expected she instantly stiffened, and he winced when her clenched fist made sharp contact with his ribs. He should have known from her vibrant hair and flashing green eyes that she was a hellcat, he thought ruefully. But the feel of her lithe body squirming against his as she struggled to escape from his grasp heated his blood and fired up his pride. He wasn't used to women resisting him. Most women he met were a little too keen for him to take them to bed—which perhaps explained his recent restlessness as he searched for an elusive something that he did not even understand. It was a long time since he had felt the thrill of the chase or had to per-suade a woman to kiss him back, but Jess had clamped her lips together in a tight line and the challenge of drawing a response from her was too strong to resist.

She had accused Drago of being a bully, but she had not expected him to prove it by kissing her against her will, Jess thought bitterly. She was furious that he had chosen to use his superior size and strength to control her. He was holding her so tightly that she could not move and was unable to jab her fist into him again. Her breasts were crushed against his chest, and the feel of his warm body through his silk shirt, together with the slight friction created as she struggled to pull herself free, was making her nipples feel hot and hard.

Dear heaven, what was happening to her? When had her determination to get away from him changed to desire? One minute she had been resisting him with all her strength, but now a curious lassitude was stealing through her and her body was sinking into him, her soft curves melting against the hardness of his thighs.

Her mouth felt bruised from his savage assault, but the nature of the kiss was changing. His lips were no longer demanding her submission but gently coaxing a response from her that she found impossible to deny. His warm breath filled her mouth as she parted her lips, and she tasted him when he dipped his tongue into her moist interior. His gentleness was unexpected and utterly beguiling. Sexual desire was something she had been sure she would never experience again, but as Drago cupped her bottom and pulled her so close that her pelvis was in direct contact with the hard ridge of his arousal straining beneath his jeans liquid heat coursed through her veins. With a soft moan Jess slid her hands to his shoulders and kissed him with the fiery passion that had lain dormant inside her for so long.

'You see, honey, I told you they were just having a lovers' tiff.'

The voice of one of the American tourists broke the silence. His companions' laughter faded with the sound of their footsteps as they continued on their way. But the comment hurtled Jess back to reality and with a low cry she tore her mouth from Drago's. To her relief he let her go, and she had a feeling that he was as shocked as she was by the chemistry that had exploded between them. He raked a hand through his dark hair, sweeping it back from his brow, and the moonlight slanting across his face struck the sharp lines of his cheekbones and revealed his tense expression.

'That shouldn't have happened,' he said harshly.

Inexplicably, Jess felt hurt by his words. Of *course* the kiss had been a mistake, a moment of madness, but by pointing it out he made her feel cheap, and the self-disgust she had heard in his voice was a shameful reminder of his low opinion of her.

She wished she could think of something sarcastic to say, but she had never been clever with words. Drago was staring at her as if he couldn't believe he had kissed her, and the disdainful curl of his lip was the final humiliation. She had to leave—now, before she felt any worse. She was furious with herself for responding to his kiss with such shameful enthusiasm.

The path running beside the canal did not continue past the end of the *palazzo*, and the American tourists had now had to retrace their steps back across the bridge. That meant the bridge was her only route of escape. But as she headed towards it Drago stepped in front of her, blocking her way.

'Come back to the house,' he ordered.

'You must be kidding.' Frantic to get away from him, she ran out along the jetty to where his boat was moored, realising as she did so how stupid the action was. She didn't know how to start the boat. As she glanced over her shoulder and saw him following she knew she was trapped. 'Leave me alone.' She held out a hand to ward him off.

'*Dio*, I'm not going to hurt you.' Drago's voice grew sharp. 'Jess—be careful!'

But his words were too late. In the dark, she hadn't realised how close she was to the end of the jetty, and with a cry she slipped and plunged into the inky depths of the canal.

CHAPTER FOUR

JESS WAS SUFFOCATING. Water filled her mouth and nose as she sank deeper. The water was so cold that her limbs, her brain, felt numb. An instinct for survival kicked in and she began to scrabble desperately against the blackness engulfing her. Her backpack was weighing her down. In panic she tore her arms free from the straps.

And then miraculously something jerked her back to the surface and she was able to drag oxygen into her lungs.

'I can't swim!' she gasped, terrified that she would sink back down again.

'It's all right. I've got you. *Santa Madre!* Stop flapping like a stranded fish and let me pull you out.'

Strong hands hauled her up and dumped her onto the jetty. Choking up the foul-tasting water she had swallowed, Jess collapsed in a heap, shudders running through her as her terror gradually receded. Pushing her tangled wet hair out of her eyes she glared at Drago. 'Of course I was damned well flapping—I thought I was going to drown.'

'You can thank me for saving you later,' he said drily. He frowned when her teeth began to chatter. The water in the canal was cold, but he assessed that the shivers racking her body were more likely due to shock. Without another word he bent and lifted her into his arms, taking no notice of her protests.

'What about my rucksack? It's still in the canal.'

'And there it will stay—unless you want to dive back in and retrieve it.'

'I told you. I can't swim.' Jess stared at Drago's implacable face with a rising sense of frustration. 'My passport is in that bag.'

'Then it's lucky you won't need it for a while,' he drawled. 'Not until Angelo has regained consciousness and the matter of his missing money has been resolved.'

A new feeling of panic swept through Jess at the prospect of being Drago's prisoner. 'You can't force me to stay,' she muttered, struggling to speak when she was shivering so hard she felt as though her bones would snap.

'I don't see how you can leave without your passport,' was his laconic reply—which ignited Jess's temper so that she renewed her efforts to force him to put her down. Drago simply tightened his hold on her and growled, 'Keep still. You've already got me wet enough. *Dio*, you're as slippery as an eel.'

Charming. That was twice in the space of a few minutes that he'd likened her to a fish! Jess knew she should continue to struggle, but she felt so tired and cold, and being carried in Drago's strong arms was dangerously seductive. Besides, where could she go now that her rucksack, containing her clothes, money and passport, was at the bottom of the canal? In a game of chess Drago would have her at checkmate, she acknowledged wearily.

He strode into the house and carried her up two flights of stairs as if she weighed nothing. Shouldering a door, he walked into a room that Jess guessed was the master suite. The elegant sitting room was decorated in shades of cream and gold and furnished with burgundy velvet sofas, and exquisite patterned rugs on the floor. But Jess only had a glimpse of the room as Drago continued on through a set of double doors into the bedroom.

Her eyes were immediately drawn to an enormous four-poster bed with gold damask drapes. The room, in particular the bed, was designed for seduction, she thought, as she took in the exotic décor of burgundy silk wallpaper. The satin bedspread was in the same rich shade.

With a renewed sense of panic she tried again to struggle out of his arms. 'Why have you brought me here? I'd like to go back to my room.'

'Not a hope. I'm not going to hang around under your balcony waiting to catch you when you take another leap out of the window.'

'I didn't leap out. It was a carefully planned escape, which I wouldn't have needed to attempt if you hadn't locked me in,' Jess snapped, stung by his scathing tone. 'And I wouldn't have fallen if you hadn't startled me. What are you doing?' she demanded when he carried her into the *en suite* bathroom and set her down in the shower cubicle. She gasped when he activated the shower and she was hit by a deluge of warm water. Her jeans and tee shirt were already wet from where she had fallen into the canal, but within seconds of standing beneath the spray her clothes were plastered to her body.

'Do you need any help getting undressed?'

'No!' She glared at Drago, incensed by his mocking smile. Following his gaze, she glanced down and was horrified to see that her thin shirt had become almost transparent and the hard points of her nipples were plainly visible through the sodden material. 'Go to hell,' she muttered, hating him—but hating her body more, for its traitorous response to his virile sex appeal.

Unexpectedly, the stricken look in Jess's eyes caused Drago a pang of remorse. Beneath her defiance she looked young and scared, and the realisation that she might be frightened of him made him uncomfortable. *Dio*, the idea of frightening a woman was abhorrent to him. He had behaved like a brute tonight, he acknowledged heavily. His concern for his cousin and the fact that he'd had barely any sleep in seventy-two hours had clouded his judgement. Although he suspected that Jess knew more about Angelo's missing inheritance fund than she was letting on, nothing had been proved—and he could not forget how convincing she had sounded when she had protested her innocence.

'Remain under the shower until you've warmed up,' he said roughly. 'I'll find something for you to wear to sleep in.'

Ten minutes later, when Jess cautiously peered around the shower screen, she was relieved to find she was alone. A pile of towels had been left for her, and a man's white shirt that she guessed belonged to Drago. He had been right about the shower warming her up—she had a feeling he was right about most things, she thought ruefully. But at least she had stopped shivering and her hair no longer smelled of canal water.

The shirt was so big on her that it reached halfway down her thighs. After blasting her hair with the dryer hanging on the wall, she acknowledged that she could not remain in the bathroom for ever.

The first thing she noticed when she opened

the door was that Drago had changed out of his damp clothes into a navy blue silk robe that revealed an expanse of broad, tanned chest overlaid with whorls of dark hair.

'Feeling better?' he queried when Jess edged into the bedroom.

She nodded, her heart jolting against her ribs as he walked over to her and handed her a glass.

'Drink this—a shot of brandy will warm your insides.'

'No, thanks. I never touch spirits.' She jerked back from him, blanching as she smelled the alcohol.

'I'm not trying to poison you,' he said drily.

'I'm sorry.' She flushed as she realised how rude she must seem. 'I loathe alcohol. Even the smell of it reminds me...'

'Reminds you of what?' Drago prompted, puzzled by her strange reaction.

'Nothing.' Jess bit her lip when she realised Drago was waiting for her to answer. 'My dad used to drink...a lot,' she muttered. 'He was an alcoholic. He drank rum, mainly, although he wasn't fussy. He'd drink anything. Our house used to stink of alcohol.'

Drago hesitated, struggling for the first time in his life to know what to say. Jess's voice had been expressionless, but he sensed that she kept a tight hold on her emotions. 'You said your father *used* to drink?' he said after a moment. 'Does that mean he is no longer an alcoholic?'

'He's dead. He died when I was eleven.'

'That must have been hard for you—to lose your father when you were so young.'

She shrugged. 'To be honest he wasn't a great dad. I don't remember him ever being sober, and he used to spend all his money on drink so there was never much to eat at home.' Once again her tone was matter-of-fact, but her eyes had darkened to a deep jade colour and held a faintly haunted expression.

'What about your mother? She didn't drink too, did she?'

'I don't think so. She died when I was a baby and I have no memory of her.'

Drago frowned. Why was he interested? he asked himself. He shouldn't give a damn about Jess's background. But he could not dismiss the image of her as an undernourished, uncared-for child. 'Who brought you up after your father died?'

'I went into a children's home, which wasn't so bad. At least I had dinner every day.' Her wry smile turned into a yawn. 'Sorry, but I'm shattered. It's been an eventful day,' she said pointedly.

'Then get into bed.' He pulled back the covers and gave her a querying look when she did not move.

Jess stared at the gold silk sheets and her heart began to pound. Surely Drago was not expecting her to sleep with him? The idea was outrageous, and yet... An image flashed into her mind of lying in that bed and feeling the sensual silk against her naked flesh. Like a film playing inside her head, she pictured Drago lying next to her, his tanned torso so dark in contrast to her paleness, his wiry chest hairs feeling faintly abrasive against her breasts as he lowered himself onto her.

Dear heaven. She drew an audible breath. Where had her shocking thoughts come from? She darted a glance at him and her heart missed a beat when she saw the predatory hunger in his eyes. The realisation that she had not imagined the sexual chemistry between them was frankly terrifying.

'No way am I going to sleep with you,' she said jerkily. 'Was that why you wanted me to drink brandy—to make me more amenable?'

'Amenable!' Drago gave a harsh laugh. 'I swear you don't know the meaning of the word.'

He did not know what angered him most—her accusation that he had planned to seduce her or the fear he glimpsed in her eyes. *Dio*, she made him feel like a monster, when in fact he'd had the patience of a saint tonight.

'For your information, I have never had to get a woman drunk to persuade her to sleep with me.'

His gaze narrowed on her flushed face. She looked a whole lot better than she had when he had pulled her from the canal: no longer a drowned rat but a red-haired sexpot with her soft lips slightly parted and the swift rise and fall of her breasts betraying her agitation. But it was not fear that made the pulse at the base of her neck beat erratically—he knew women too well, and he recognised the subtle signals her body was sending him.

'I would not need to ply you with alcohol to get you into bed, would I, *cara*?' he taunted softly. 'From your response when I kissed you earlier I got the impression that I could take you any time I liked.' Ignoring her fierce denial, he continued ruthlessly, 'But someone with a conviction for fraud is not my ideal mistress. I have no intention of sharing a bed with you. The only reason I suggested you should sleep here is because you stripped the sheets from *your* bed to use in your juvenile escape attempt, and I'm not going to disturb the housemaid and ask her to prepare another bed for you. I'll sleep in my dressing room for what's left of tonight.'

As he strode past Jess on his way to his dressing room her dumbstruck expression awarded Drago some satisfaction. She was the craziest, most irritating woman he had ever met, he assured himself. But when he stretched out on the sofa bed sleep eluded him despite his tiredness, and his body ached with sexual frustration as he remembered how soft her lips had felt beneath his.

* * *

The sound of someone calling her name dragged Jess from a deep sleep, and she was vaguely aware of something lightly brushing her face. She blinked blearily as Drago's hard-boned face filled her vision, and she was instantly awake and acutely aware of him.

God, he was gorgeous, she thought ruefully. His casual clothes of yesterday had been replaced with a dark suit and crisp white shirt that contrasted starkly with his olive-toned skin. He had evidently shaved, for his jaw was smooth and she inhaled the subtle scent of sandalwood cologne.

His sensual mouth was unsmiling, and as her memory of all the previous day's events returned a sense of dread gripped her. 'Is there any news about Angelo?'

'His condition is unchanged,' he informed her in a clipped tone. 'When you've got up and had something to eat we'll go to the hospital. I still believe you are the best hope of rousing him.'

With an effort Drago moved away from the bed before he gave in to temptation and joined Jess between the sheets. She reminded him of a sleepy kitten, curled up beneath the covers, her tawny hair spread across the pillows and her cat-like green eyes watching him from beneath long silky lashes.

He had woken earlier, feeling better for a few hours' uninterrupted sleep, and more in control of himself. He'd hardly been able to believe that he had allowed a skinny redhead with an attitude problem to provoke him into losing his cool. But when he had leaned across the bed, intending to wake Jess, he had been riveted by her beautiful face. Unable to resist, he had run his finger lightly down her sleep-flushed cheek and discovered that her skin was as velvet-soft as a peach. Her lips had been slightly parted, and he'd felt a fierce longing to cover them with his own.

Cursing silently, he walked over to the window and pulled back the curtains to allow the bright April sunshine to flood the room. 'From now on you will sleep in the bedroom adjacent to mine. It does not have a balcony, so I'm afraid you won't be able to try another escape trick,' he said sardonically. 'I have also arranged for some clothes to be delivered for you as yours are at the bottom of the canal.'

Jess decided not to point out that she considered it entirely *his* fault she had lost all her belongings. He had not mentioned his threat of the previous night to hand her over to the police and she deemed it better not to antagonise him. Once Angelo had regained consciousness and explained that he had not given her his inheritance money Drago would owe her a grovelling apology, but for now, bearing in mind that she did not have a passport, she realised she had no choice but to remain in Venice with him.

'Thank you,' she murmured. 'If you give me the bill for the clothes I will, of course, pay you what I owe.'

She sounded genuine, and she looked so god-damned innocent. Drago's eyes narrowed. Were his suspicions about her wrong? How could they be when the evidence was stacked against her? Angelo had told Aunt Dorotea he had given Jess his inheritance fund, and the private investigator had confirmed that she had a criminal record for fraud. She might look as though butter wouldn't melt in her mouth but he was not fooled by her, he assured himself.

'It isn't necessary for you to pay for them. The clothes belong to me.'

Her eyes widened. 'Well, either I'm going to look pretty silly, wearing clothes designed for a six-foot man, or you're a cross-dresser.'

For a few seconds Drago could think of nothing to say in response to her startling statement, but then his lips twitched and he threw back his head and laughed. 'I promise you I don't have a penchant for dressing up in women's clothes and stiletto heels.'

He watched Jess's mouth curve into a smile and realised she had been teasing him. It was a novelty. He was not used to women with a sense of humour; most of the women he knew took themselves far too seriously. It felt strange to laugh, he mused. Even before Angelo's accident there had rarely seemed anything to laugh about recently. The responsibility of running a business empire and taking care of his family weighed heavily on him. Although he made time to play squash and work out in his private gym, and he enjoyed an active sex life with numerous mistresses, his life was dictated by work and duty and he could not remember the last time anyone had made him smile.

'The clothes are from the Cassa di Cassari collection,' he explained. 'Clothing is a new venture that the company is expanding into, and we have employed the top Italian fashion designer Torre Umberto. The new line won't be available in the shops until next month, but Torre has sent some samples over for you to wear.'

His phone rang, breaking the curious connection he had briefly felt with Jess. He headed a global business empire which demanded his constant attention. He was distracted enough, worrying about his cousin, and he definitely did not have time to be distracted by a sassy redhead whose sweet smile made his guts ache, Drago reminded himself.

'When you're ready, the maid will show you the way to the dining room,' he told her abruptly before he headed out of the door.

They had been at the hospital for hours, but still Angelo showed no sign of regaining consciousness. Jess stood up from her chair next to the bed, needing to stretch her legs. The small room felt claustrophobic, and although the blind at the window was pulled down the bright sunshine beating against the glass increased the stifling atmosphere.

As she walked over to the water dispenser and filled a plastic cup she was aware of two pairs of eyes following her. Angelo's mother was no friendlier today than she had been last night and had not spoken a word to her. The poor woman was devastated, Jess reminded herself. But she also knew that the vibes of distrust from Drago's aunt were due to her belief that Jess had conned her son out of his inheritance fund. When Angelo woke up he was going to have a hell of a lot of explaining to do, she thought heavily.

Dorotea turned her attention back to her son, but Jess was conscious that Drago's gaze was still focused on her, and she self-consciously ran a hand over the cream jersey-silk skirt that she had discovered, along with a selection of other outfits, in the wardrobe of her room at the Palazzo d'Inverno.

The last time she had worn a skirt had been

years ago, on one of the rare occasions when she had attended school, she thought wryly. She lived in jeans or work overalls, and she felt overdressed in the skirt and the delicate white blouse she had teamed with it. The tan leather belt around her waist matched the three-inch stiletto-heeled shoes. The elegant outfit had called for her to try to tame her thick hair, and she had swept it up into a loose knot on top of her head.

Staring at her reflection in the mirror before she had left her bedroom, she had been stunned by the transformation. She had always thought of her body as shapeless and too thin, but the beautifully designed skirt suited her slim figure, and the blouse was cleverly cut so that her small bust looked fuller. For the first time in years—since she was seventeen, in fact, and had worn a new dress to go out to dinner with her boss, Sebastian Loxley—she felt like an attractive woman. The glitter of sexual awareness in Drago's eyes when she had walked into the dining room at the *palazzo* had sent a thrill of feminine pride through her. He had not commented on her appearance, but she had been aware of him glancing at her several times as they had eaten breakfast—just as she was aware of him watching her now.

'I need some air,' he announced abruptly. The metal feet of his chair scraped loudly on the floor as he stood up. His eyes met Jess's, but his expression was unreadable. 'We'll go and get a coffee. You need a break,' he insisted when she opened her mouth to argue. 'You have talked to Angelo and sung to him—' he glanced briefly at the guitar standing by the bed '—almost constantly for four hours.'

'I came to try to help,' she replied huskily, feeling herself blush. She had sung a couple of pop ballads that Angelo had taught her to play on the guitar while Drago had gone to make a phone call, and she felt embarrassed that he must have been just outside the door and had heard her.

'Hopefully he will regain consciousness soon, and if he does it will be no small thanks to you,' Drago said roughly.

He could not help but be impressed by Jess's efforts to rouse his cousin. She had barely moved from his bedside since they had arrived at the hospital that morning, and she had talked to him until her throat sounded dry. The question of whether they were lovers returned to taunt him. She had denied it, had said that they were simply friends, but she was so goddamned beautiful and it was easy to believe she had seduced shy, inexperienced Angelo with her sex-kitten sensuality and persuaded him to give her a fortune.

Drago's jaw clenched. She had taken his breath away when she had joined him for breakfast at the *palazzo* that morning, dressed in clothes that had drawn his gaze to her slender but shapely figure. The scruffy tomboy had turned into an elegant woman, but beneath her new sophistication he recognised her inherently sensual nature, and his appetite for food had deserted him as he'd fantasised about having hot, hard sex with her on the dining table.

Frowning at the inappropriateness of his thoughts when his cousin was in a critical condition, Drago was unaware of how forbidding he looked as he escorted Jess to the hospital cafeteria. He ordered two coffees and carried them over to the empty table she had found.

She seemed distracted as she added three

spoons of sugar to her coffee, prompting him to ask, 'Is something wrong?'

'I wish my phone wasn't at the bottom of the canal,' she said ruefully. 'I'd like to call Mike, my foreman, to make sure the job we've been working on will be finished on time. Clients hate delays, and it's important that the company maintains a good reputation.' Jess pushed a stray tendril of hair back from her face. 'Do the doctors have any idea of when Angelo might regain consciousness? I want to stay if it is deemed that hearing my voice might help rouse him, but I have a responsibility to my team of decorators in London. If I don't finalise our next contract they won't have any work.'

Drago sipped his unsweetened black coffee, relishing the hit of caffeine, and gave her a speculative look. 'I understand that your decorating business was facing bankruptcy until a few months ago?'

'How do you know that?' Her startled expression turned to anger. 'I suppose the investigator you hired to spy on me told you?'

He did not deny it. 'I know you paid twenty

thousand pounds into the company account to clear its debts and overdraft. I can't help thinking how remarkably convenient it was that you suddenly acquired a large sum of money just in time to save the business from financial meltdown.'

As his meaning became clear, Jess felt sick. 'If you think I got the money from Angelo, you're wrong.'

'So where *did* it come from? And perhaps you can also explain how you live in a luxury apartment with a rental value far higher than you could afford on a decorator's wage.'

Jess was stunned at how much he knew about her personal life, and felt violated by the intrusion.

'I don't have to explain anything to you,' she said angrily. 'But as a matter of fact the money I used to bail out T&J Decorators was left to me.'

Drago looked disbelieving. 'You're saying you received an inheritance? Who from? You told me your alcoholic father spent all his money on drink.'

'Yeah, *he* certainly never gave me anything— not even affection,' Jess said bitterly. 'Have you any idea what it's like to be the only child in the class not to be dressed in clean clothes? Or the only one not to go on a school trip because your dad was too drunk to sign the permission form?' She clamped her lips together, startled by her outburst. Her childhood was something she *never* spoke about. 'Of course you don't know. You were born into a wealthy, loving family.'

She swallowed. 'I didn't know what it felt like to be part of a family until I was seventeen, when I went to stay with a wonderful couple who had experience of helping troubled teenagers. Ted and Margaret changed my life in so many ways. Sadly they are both dead now, and six months ago I learned that I was a beneficiary in Margaret's will.'

The raw emotion in Jess's voice tugged on Drago's insides. He was shocked by her revelations about her childhood and felt uncomfortable that his questioning of her had forced her to talk about a subject she clearly found painful. She could be making up a sob story to gain his sympathy, his mind pointed out. But the haunted expression in her eyes was too real to be an act.

'As for how I afford to live in an expensive

property,' she continued, 'I have an arrangement with a property developer who allows me to live in properties he owns rent-free. In return I carry out renovation work and decorate them to a high standard. As soon as the work is finished on the flat I'm currently living in I'll move out, and the developer will lease it to paying tenants.'

Jess glared at Drago. 'You are wrong about me,' she said fiercely. 'And when Angelo wakes up and tells you where his money is I'll expect an apology from you.'

His coldly arrogant expression did not soften. 'I'm not wrong about your criminal record. It is an undeniable fact that you were convicted of fraud, and in light of that I think my suspicion that you know what has happened to my cousin's inheritance is understandable.'

'I was seventeen, for God's sake, and very naïve.' Jess bit her lip. 'I was set up and I didn't understand that I was committing a crime.'

'Set up by whom?'

The rank disbelief in Drago's tone made Jess's heart sink. She had no chance of convincing him of her innocence when she had þeen found guilty by a jury, she acknowledged bleakly. The injustice of what had happened still burned inside her. But at the same time as the court case seven years ago, she had had to make a monumental decision that had left her feeling numb and strangely distanced from other events in her life.

'Explain what you mean about being set up,' Drago demanded.

'What's the point?' She tore her eyes from his hard-boned face, hating the way her body responded to him. 'You have already judged me. The only person who can exonerate me is Angelo.'

The strident ring of his phone made them both jump. Drago frowned when he saw the hospital consultant's number flash on the caller display, and he quickly answered. After a terse conversation in Italian he ended the call and stared across the table at Jess.

'Angelo has just regained consciousness—and he has asked for you.'

CHAPTER FIVE

THEY WERE MET at the door of the intensive care unit by a smartly dressed woman whom Drago hurriedly introduced as his mother. Luisa Cassari subjected Jess to a sharp stare, which became speculative as she turned her gaze on her son.

'I thought the new Cassari clothing range wasn't going to be launched in stores until May, but I see Miss Harper is already wearing pieces from the collection.'

Drago met his mother's enquiry coolly. 'It was necessary to provide Jess with something to wear after she lost all her belongings.'

Her brows rose as she glanced back at Jess. 'How did you lose your things?'

'Um…I fell into the canal.' Jess felt her face burning. 'It's a long story,' she mumbled.

'And an intriguing one, I'm sure.'

There followed a rapid conversation in Italian

between mother and son, and Jess was surprised to see that Drago looked faintly uncomfortable.

'We should be concentrating on Angelo,' he told his mother, reverting back to English and speaking in a firm tone that caused Luisa to compress her lips. But she made no further comment as Drago placed his hand on Jess's shoulder and pushed her towards the bed.

Aunt Dorotea was gripping Angelo's hand while tears streamed down her face.

Drago spoke to the doctor who was standing nearby. 'What's happened?'

'He came round a few minutes ago and asked for his mother. He was lucid, and the signs are good that he is emerging from the coma.' The doctor looked at Jess. 'He also murmured *your* name. I think it would help if he heard your voice.'

Supremely conscious that everyone in the room was watching her, Jess leaned over the bed and said softly, 'Hi, Angelo. It's great to have you back.'

His eyelids fluttered and slowly opened. 'Jess?'

'Yeah, it's me.' Tears clogged her throat so that

her voiced emerged as a croaky whisper. She felt weak with relief that Angelo was back from the brink.

His eyes had closed, but now they opened again. 'What happened to me?'

After darting a questioning glance at the doctor, Jess said gently, 'You had a car accident. Do you remember?'

Angelo's brow furrowed. 'No,' he said at last. 'I needed to tell Drago something...but I don't remember what it was.' He focused unsteadily on Jess and managed a faint smile. 'I know that we are friends.' His smile faded. 'But I don't remember how I know you. I don't remember anything...except that I had to see Drago urgently.'

'I'm here,' Drago said gruffly, struggling to control his emotions. 'Take it easy, Angelo. I'm sure your memory will come back soon.'

Angelo turned his head on the pillow and smiled at his mother. *'Ciao, Mamma.'*

Aunt Dorotea promptly burst into tears again, and as she leaned across the bed to kiss her son Drago indicated that Jess should step back.

'Aren't you going to ask him about his inheritance money?' she demanded in a fierce whisper, while the doctor and nursing staff crowded around the bed.

'He's hardly in a fit state. You heard what he said. He doesn't remember anything at the moment. I need to have a word with the doctor about Angelo's memory loss.'

Drago followed the consultant out of the room, and when he returned a few minutes later his expression was grim. Angelo had fallen into a peaceful sleep, and Drago spoke in a low voice.

'The consultant says that amnesia after a head injury is fairly common, but he can't predict how long it will last. There are some other issues that he is more concerned about—particularly the serious break to Angelo's left leg, which will require surgery.' His aunt gasped, and he put his arm around her shoulders. 'Try not to worry,' he told her gently. 'The doctor says he will be fine, and he is sure that in time his memory will return. A brain scan will tell us more. But for now we must be patient, and not excite or upset Angelo in any way that could hinder his recovery.'

He looked at Jess as he made this last statement, the hard expression in his black eyes warning her not to say anything until they had moved away from Angelo's bedside. Holding open the door, he waited for her to precede him out into the corridor.

'The consultant believes you could be the key to Angelo regaining his memory,' he told her. 'The fact that he remembers you, but not the accident, means that the amnesia is patchy, and if you keep talking to him you may jog his memory into returning fully.'

But until his memory did return *she* was still under suspicion from Drago and the other members of Angelo's family, who believed she had persuaded him to give her a fortune, Jess realised heavily. 'It could take days, or even weeks before he regains his memory.' A note of panic crept into her voice. 'You can't possibly expect me to stay in Venice indefinitely.'

'That's exactly what I expect,' Drago said coolly. 'Angelo's mind is trapped at a point in time when he believes you are his friend. When his memory eventually returns he may be able to explain why he told his mother that he gave you his inheritance fund and the truth of the matter will be revealed. But until then you will stay at the Palazzo d'Inverno as my guest.'

'As your prisoner, you mean,' she said angrily. 'Guests aren't usually locked in their room. Much as I want to help, I can't abandon my business.' She felt bad about leaving Angelo, but her team of workmen relied on her. 'I'm sorry, but I have to go back to London.'

Drago's dark brows lifted in the arrogant expression Jess was becoming familiar with. 'How do you intend to do that without a passport or money?'

'I suppose I'll have to go to the British Embassy and report that I've lost my passport.' In truth she did not have a clue how she was going to get home, but she did not want him to guess she was worried.

'You don't even have money to pay for a taxi to the airport, much less an air ticket to London,' he pointed out. 'You should be grateful that I have offered you somewhere to stay.'

The mockery in his voice ignited Jess's temper. 'Grateful? I'd rather take my chances in a pit of rattlesnakes than stay with you.' Her voice rose as she forgot that they were standing outside Angelo's room, within earshot of Drago's mother and aunt, not to mention half a dozen medical staff. Fury flashed in her green eyes. 'You are a dictatorial, egotistical—' She broke off and gave a startled gasp when his arm shot around her waist and he dragged her hard up against him. Too late she realised that she had pushed him beyond the limits of his patience.

'And *you* have viper's tongue,' Drago growled, before he silenced her by bringing his mouth down on hers in a punishing kiss designed to prove his dominance.

Determined not to respond, Jess clamped her lips together, but her senses were swamped by the tantalising scent of his aftershave and the feel of his smooth cheek brushing against hers. His warm breath filled her mouth as he teased her lips apart with his tongue, probing insistently until with a low moan she sank against him, a prisoner to his masterful passion. But he was as much a slave to the explosive sexual chemistry that burned like a white-hot flame between them as she was, she realised, when he cupped her bottom and pulled her into the cradle of his thighs, so that she was intensely aware of his powerful erection.

His breathing was ragged when he finally tore his mouth from hers, and the savage glitter in his eyes echoed the harshness of his voice. '*Madonna*, I think you must be a witch. You are driving me crazy.' His lip curled with self-disgust. 'My cousin has serious injuries, the extent of which are not fully known, yet all I can think about is how goddamned beautiful you are and how badly I want you.'

Jess was shaken to hear him admit he was attracted to her. But rather than feeling triumphant that a man as gorgeous and sexy as Drago desired her she was afraid of where their mutual awareness might lead, and terrified that she would be unable to resist him if he kissed her again.

'Let me go,' she pleaded huskily. 'If you help me get to England I'll repay you the cost of my flight, and I promise I'll come back to visit Angelo.'

He gave a harsh laugh. 'I'm not letting you out

of my sight until I find out what happened to my cousin's inheritance.'

The door to Angelo's room suddenly opened, making them spring apart. But not quickly enough to escape Drago's mother's keen scrutiny. Jess's mouth felt swollen and her breasts ached with a sweet heaviness. A glance downwards revealed that her nipples were plainly visible, jutting beneath the fine material of her blouse. She hastily crossed her arms in front of her, blushing furiously when Luisa stared at her and then at her son.

'Angelo would like to see you,' she said to Jess. 'If you are not busy?' she added, in a tone as dry as a desert.

'I'll come and sit with him,' she mumbled. She felt humiliated by the look of disdain in Luisa Cassari's eyes, but Drago seemed indifferent to his mother's disapproval. He was reading a message he had received on his phone and then glanced briefly at Jess.

'I need to go to the office for a couple of hours. When you have spent some time with Angelo my bodyguard will take you back to the *palazzo*.'

As he spoke the stocky man who had met them at the airport the previous day walked down the corridor towards them. Fico planted himself outside Angelo's room and crossed his arms over his massive chest.

'He doesn't speak a word of English,' Drago murmured. 'And he is under strict orders to escort you from the hospital straight to my house.'

Anger surged through her. 'In other words he's my jailer?'

He gave a laconic shrug of his broad shoulders. 'Don't be so melodramatic. I'll see you at dinner tonight.'

'I can't wait,' Jess muttered sarcastically. As she turned away from him and marched into Angelo's room she was unaware of a flare of amusement and grudging admiration in Drago's eyes.

Much later that night, Drago strode through the Palazzo d'Inverno, his solitary footsteps echoing hollowly on the marble staircase. It was not the first time he had instructed the household staff not to wait up for him, nor the first time he had missed dinner because he'd had to deal with a crisis at work.

No doubt Jess would have been glad of his absence this evening, he mused. She had already left the hospital with Fico by the time he had arrived to visit his cousin and meet with Angelo's medical team. The young man's injuries were serious, and he faced a long road back to recovery, but thank God he had not suffered brain damage. The brain scan had revealed severe bruising, and there was the worry of his memory loss, but there was every reason to hope that the amnesia would be short-lived. Once Angelo's memory had returned hopefully he would shed some light on the matter of his missing inheritance fund and confirm if he had given the money to Jess—something she strenuously denied.

Madonna! How had she crept into his mind again? Drago asked himself angrily. He had accused her of being a witch. Perhaps she really was a sorceress and had cast a spell on him? Even during the emergency board meeting he'd chaired to discuss a problem that had arisen with a new project in China he had struggled to keep his thoughts from wandering to the sassy, sexy redhead who was currently a guest or a prisoner at his home, depending on your viewpoint.

Jess had made her feelings very clear, he thought wryly. She had antagonised him until he had kissed her, but when she had kissed him back his anger had turned to scorching desire. For the rest of the day he had been able to taste her on his lips, and the lingering scent of her perfume still tormented him. Guilt assailed him that Jess dominated his thoughts, but he was relieved to know for certain that she and his cousin were not lovers. Angelo had given him a curious look when Drago had asked him about his relationship with Jess, but had explained that they were simply friends.

The chef had left a platter of cold meats and salad in the fridge for him. Drago carried his supper up to his room, his footsteps slowing as he walked past Jess's bedroom and saw light filtering beneath the door. Ignoring the temptation to check if she was awake, he carried on into his suite of rooms, flicked on the TV and forced himself to eat even though he had no appetite—

at least not for food, he acknowledged, aware of a tightening sensation in his groin as an image of Jess lying naked on his bed flooded his mind.

Muttering a curse, he put down the plate and headed into the *en suite* bathroom, hoping that a shower would help to relieve his tension.

Jess felt too wound up to sleep. She lay in bed, staring up at the ceiling which, like in the first room she had occupied, before her ill-fated attempt to climb down from the balcony, was decorated with elaborate artwork. But even though the fresco depicting the goddess Aphrodite was beautiful she was bored with studying it—just as she was bored with watching television when all the programmes were in Italian.

Her mind returned to wondering why Drago had not returned to the *palazzo* for dinner. Not that she had wanted to spend time with him, and she certainly hadn't changed into a gorgeous green silk dress from the Cassa di Cassari collection because she had hoped to impress him, but she had felt strangely lonely sitting on her own at the huge polished dining table. And that really did not make sense, because after growing up in the children's home constantly surrounded by other kids she liked her own company.

Drago had probably gone to visit a girlfriend. It was inconceivable that a man as devastatingly handsome and sexy as he was did not have a lover—or maybe more than one. Good luck to them, she thought as she sat up and thumped her pillows. Any woman who took him on would have to cope with his arrogant and bossy nature.

A sudden crash, followed by a shout, shattered the silence. The sounds had been loud, even through the walls that separated her room from Drago's, and the deathly quiet that followed seemed ominous to Jess's overactive imagination. Curiosity got the better of her and she slid out of bed.

The door to Drago's suite was shut. She knocked, but received no answer, and after a moment's hesitation she turned the handle and found that the door was unlocked. Her bare feet made no sound on the carpet as she crossed the sitting room. The door leading to his bedroom was ajar, and as she cautiously peeped round it she inhaled an over-whelmingly strong scent of aftershave.

Just then he emerged from the *en suite* bathroom, and the sight of his blood-soaked chest caused her to give a sharp cry.

'Santa Madre!' He stopped dead, clearly shocked to see her. 'What are you doing, flitting around the house as noiselessly as a wraith?'

'I heard a crash…' Jess could not tear her eyes from what she now realised was a blood-stained towel wrapped around the hand that he was holding against his chest. 'What have you done?'

He glanced down at his front and said wryly, 'It's not as bad as it looks. I cut my hand on some glass and it's made a bloody mess—literally. I knocked a bottle of cologne into the sink and then compounded my clumsiness by trying to pick up the shards of glass. The damned cut won't stop bleeding. Can you look in the bathroom cabinet for a bandage?' He gave her an intent look when she hesitated. 'Does the sight of blood bother you?'

No way was Jess going to admit that it was not the blood that bothered her but the sight of Drago's naked, olive-skinned chest as he shrugged off his stained shirt. Her gaze was drawn to the hard ridges of his abdominal muscles, and followed the path of wiry black hair that arrowed down his torso and disappeared beneath the waistband of his trousers.

She swallowed, and replied in a faintly strained voice, 'No. When I was a kid I regularly used to patch my dad up after he'd had some accident or other while he was drunk. Once he fell through a neighbour's greenhouse and was cut to ribbons.'

Drago frowned. 'How old were you when that happened?'

She shrugged. 'Eight or so. Sit down while I dress the wound,' she bade him, when she had followed him into the bathroom and found a medical box in the cupboard.

He sat on the edge of the bath and unwound the towel to reveal a deep cut across his palm. 'I've kept pressure on it and elevated my hand. The bleeding seems to be easing.'

'I don't think it needs stitching,' Jess said after she had inspected the wound. 'You're lucky.'

'*Sì.*' He could not disguise the weariness in his

voice. 'I don't fancy another trip to the hospital tonight.'

She threw him a quick look. 'Is that where you've been? I wondered why you weren't at dinner.'

'Why, *cara*, you almost sound as though you missed me,' he drawled.

'Of course I didn't. Why would I miss my jailer?' Aware that she was blushing, she concentrated on her task. 'At least the cut will have been sterilised by the cologne,' she murmured as she began to bandage his hand. 'It smells like a sultan's harem in here.'

'Are you speaking from personal experience?'

Drago subjected her to a leisurely inspection that for some reason made her feel hot and shivery at the same time.

'I'm sure you would be a sultan's favourite concubine, with your creamy skin and fiery hair,' he said softly.

Startled by the sudden change in his voice, from teasing to husky and achingly sensual, Jess caught her breath. Her eyes flew to his, and saw the undisguised hunger in his glittering stare. 'Of course I've never been in a harem,' she choked. 'I would never be a man's plaything. I believe in equality between men and women.'

Nothing on earth would make her confess her secret fantasy of being swept into the arms of a handsome, powerful man and being seduced on silken sheets. In the fantasy she fought against his dominance at first, but she could not resist the skilful touch of his hands and mouth as he aroused her and tormented her until she begged for him to possess her.

Her dream lover had never had a face—until now. She darted a glance at Drago's chiselled features and felt her stomach dip. He was all her fantasies rolled into one, she acknowledged ruefully. His hard-boned masculine beauty was made even sexier by the shadow of dark stubble on his jaw. She stared at his mouth, remembering how it had felt on hers when he had kissed her, and unconsciously she wet her lips with the tip of her tongue, as if she could recapture the taste of him.

The atmosphere in the bathroom altered subtly and the sexual tension was almost palpable. Drago was conscious of the slow thud of his heart, and even more aware of the throbbing ache in his groin, the urgent drumbeat of desire flooding through his veins. It had started with the brush of Jess's fingers on his skin as she'd wrapped the bandage around his hand. The contrast of her pale fingers against his darkly tanned flesh had made him imagine her naked in his arms, her smooth white limbs entwined with his hair-roughened thighs.

But in all honesty it had started before that— when she had appeared in his room looking utterly delectable, wearing a nightgown from the Cassa di Cassari collection that was little more than a wisp of white silk and lace. She was an intriguing mixture of virginal innocence and sensual siren, with her crushed-berry lips and those startling green cat's eyes.

As she leaned over him to tend to his hand he breathed in the delicate rose-scented fragrance of her skin, and the brush of her silky hair against his bare shoulder inflamed his senses. From the first moment he had seen her in London he had felt a primitive hunger to possess her and claim her as his woman. He was no Neanderthal; he was a twenty-first century guy who believed in equality between the sexes as much as she did. But his desire for her was a pagan force he had no control over.

He had never wanted any woman the way he wanted Jess, Drago acknowledged. The gentle concern in her eyes as she tied the bandage on his hand called to something deep inside him. Since the death of his father he had been the carer and protector of his family, always strong and in control. Tonight that control was slipping away from him. He was not thinking about his suspicion that she was involved with his cousin's missing inheritance fund, or that she had once been convicted of fraud. All he could think of was that her glorious red-gold hair felt like silk when he brushed it back from her face, and her rose-flushed cheek was velvet-soft beneath his fingertips.

Driven purely by instinct, he threaded his fingers through her hair and drew her head towards him. He was still sitting on the edge of the bath, and her petite stature meant that her face was level with his and her lips were tantalisingly close. She did not resist or pull away, but he could hear the catch of her breath and see the pulse at the base of her throat beating frantically. For a few seconds they remained poised while anticipation built to an intolerable level. Their eyes locked and held, until with a harsh groan Drago slanted his mouth over hers and kissed her with slow deliberation that quickly flared into a firestorm of passion.

Drago's tongue probed expertly between Jess's lips to coax them apart—although in truth he did not need to do much coaxing, she acknowledged ruefully. From the moment he had captured her mouth she had been lost, and with no thought in her head to deny him she parted her lips and heard him give a low groan as he explored her inner sweetness.

He was the man of her fantasies. The only man she had ever allowed to breach her defences since Seb. The memory of that disastrous relationship made her stiffen and question what she was doing. Drago had openly stated that he mistrusted her. Why, then, was she allowing him to kiss her? And why was she responding to him?

Because she could not help herself, whispered a little voice inside her head. Because the very first time she had seen him she had felt that she belonged in some deep and fundamental way to him. Her sensible self knew it was ridiculous; she did not need to belong to anyone, and she knew how dangerous it was to want to be cared for. She had fallen for Seb because she had been lonely and desperate to be loved. But he had abused her trust and she had vowed never to risk her heart again.

Drago finally broke the kiss and Jess knew she should pull out of his arms and end the madness. She knew it, but she could not do it. He trailed his lips over her cheek, her throat, and she shivered with pleasure when he found the sensitive place behind her ear.

'*Cara*, you are so beautiful,' he said raggedly, and his deeply sensual voice made her shiver again with a fierce, sharp need that started low in her belly and radiated through her so that every nerve-ending on her body felt acutely sensitive.

He captured the pulse throbbing at the base of her throat and then brushed his mouth along her collarbone. Her heart stopped when he slid the strap of her nightgown over her shoulder. Her breasts ached with a sweet heaviness, and when he brushed his fingers over the swollen peaks of her nipples, straining beneath the silk, she jerked as if an electrical current had shot through her.

He gave a husky laugh, but there was no amusement in eyes that were as black as jet and glittering with predatory intent. 'I know. It's the same for me too. The wanting. The hunger clawing in my gut.'

His jaw tightened and Jess sensed he was fighting an internal battle with himself, as if he resented his desire for her.

'When you opened the door of your flat in London I took one look at you and knew I had to have you,' he admitted in a driven tone.

'Drago…' Jess gave a keening cry when he tugged her nightgown lower and bared one of her breasts.

He stared at her, tension in every sculpted line of his face, his skin stretched tight over his sharp cheekbones. 'No games,' he said harshly. 'If you don't want this then go—now.'

He did not try to persuade her to stay with words and promises that they both knew would be false, and Jess was glad of that. She had been fooled by promises once before and her heart had been broken as a consequence. She was not a vulnerable seventeen-year-old any more, she reminded herself. She had grown up and discarded her silly dreams. Sexual desire was a perfectly natural feeling, and there was nothing wrong with wanting to give in to its demands. As long as she remembered to keep her head screwed on her heart would be in no danger.

CHAPTER SIX

'WE BARELY KNOW each other.' An instinct for self-protection made Jess cling to the last shreds of her sanity and offer a valid reason why she should walk away from Drago. 'And what you think you know about me isn't the truth,' she added, unable to hide the bitterness in her voice.

'Maybe it isn't.' As he uttered the words, Drago accepted that he did not know what to think about her.

He had evidence that she had been convicted of fraud, but it had happened a long time ago, when she had been a teenager. A mistake in her past did not mean she was inherently untrustworthy, his mind argued. *Madonna*, was he making excuses for her because he needed to justify his desire for her? He still did not understand what her true involvement with his cousin was, but she had fiercely denied knowing anything about Angelo's missing inheritance fund.

He did not know what to believe, and right now—shocking though it was to admit it—he did not care about his cousin, or the money, or anything that had happened in Jess's past. All he cared about was that she was half-naked and so exquisitely lovely that simply looking at her made him harder than he had ever been in his life. His hand actually shook as he reached out and slid the other strap of her nightgown down her arm, until her small, firm breasts with their dusky pink nipples were revealed to his hungry gaze.

'It's true we don't know many details about each other, but from the moment we met we were both aware of the chemistry that exists between us. No other woman has ever made me feel this out of control,' Drago admitted roughly. 'Say something, damn it,' he growled, feeling his blood pound through his veins when she simply stared at him with her stunning green eyes. Witch's eyes, trapping him in her spell.

He didn't care. Nothing mattered but the feel of her silken skin as he clasped her shoulders and pulled her to him. Nothing mattered but the hon-eyed taste of her as he lowered his head and captured her mouth in a potent kiss that demanded a response she gave so willingly that he could not restrain a husky groan when he felt her lips part obediently, allowing him to thrust his tongue between them.

Jess's heart thudded hard against her ribs when Drago suddenly stood up from the edge of the bath and scooped her into his arms as if she was a rag doll. She felt as boneless as one, she thought ruefully. One kiss was all it had taken to turn the sharp-tongued firebrand Jess Harper she prided herself on being into a trembling mass of nervous excitement. Drago was going to make love to her, and she was not going to stop him.

He carried her through to his bedroom. As her gaze fell on the four-poster bed, with its opulent gold silk drapes and sheets, the dull ache in the pit of her stomach became an insistent throb and she was conscious of molten warmth between her thighs. He placed her on the bed and stared down at her with a brooding intensity in his black eyes that was just as arousing as if he had touched her.

'I want to make love to you slowly—indulge in leisurely foreplay and prolong the pleasure until one of us begs for release,' he bit out. 'But I am so turned on that there isn't a chance in hell of that happening, *mia bella*.'

His taut voice revealed that he was hanging onto his self-control with supreme effort. Amazed that she could have such an effect on him, Jess touched the nerve jumping in his cheek. Her heart leapt when he turned his head so that his mouth grazed her fingers.

'I want you too,' she whispered.

It was what Drago wanted to hear, and his body reacted predictably. But the faint hesitancy he heard in her voice made him hold back from ripping off her nightgown and pushing her legs apart so that he could take her hard and fast, as the blood pounding in his veins urged him to do. She was not behaving as he had expected her to. His previous sexual encounters had always been with experienced women, who knew how to please him and were not shy about stating what pleased them. But Jess was clearly waiting for him to take the lead.

She looked incredibly sexy, stretched out on the bed with her fiery hair spread over the pillows, her small, pale breasts with their tightly puckered pink nipples practically begging for the ministrations of his tongue. And yet at the same time he sensed an innocence about her that made him think that she had not had many lovers.

Why the idea should make him want to grin he did not know, but as he smiled at her and watched her lips curve in a tentative response he felt a curious tug on his insides, and he forced himself to relax and slow the pace a little.

'Show me how much you want me,' he murmured as he bent his head and slanted his mouth over hers. Her immediate response stoked his desire, and he groaned and deepened the kiss until he felt tremors run through her body and realised that he was shaking too.

He heard the faint catch of her breath when he stroked her breasts, and the soft moan she gave as he flicked his thumb-pads across her nipples made him want to drag her beneath him and seek the release he craved. She was so sweetly responsive, and yet he sensed she was surprised by his caresses, as if the sensations she felt when he kissed her and touched her body were new to her.

From then on Drago forgot his own needs and concentrated on arousing Jess. He breathed in the delicate fragrance of her skin as he kissed her throat, the creamy slopes of her breasts, and finally closed his lips around one taut, dusky peak and then its twin. Her nightgown was bunched up around her waist, and he pushed it over her hips and placed his hand over the slight mound of her womanhood, hidden from his gaze beneath the fragile barrier of white lace knickers. She gave an involuntary movement and tried to clamp her legs together, but released her breath on a shivery sigh when he gently eased her thighs apart and slid his fingers beneath her panties. With delicate precision he dipped a finger into her moist opening and felt her buck her hips as he probed deeper into her honeyed sweetness.

Jess trembled as Drago continued his intimate exploration. She had never experienced such intense pleasure as he was eliciting, with his wickedly inventive fingers and with his mouth as he bent his head to her breasts and lashed her swollen nipples with his tongue. Sex with Seb had been very different, she thought ruefully. The few times she had slept with him he had seemed far more intent on his own pleasure than hers, but she had been so besotted with him that she'd felt grateful for any small sign of affection from him.

She was jolted from her thoughts of the past when Drago stood up from the bed and stripped off the rest of his clothes. Black silk boxers followed his trousers to the floor, and the sight of his naked, hugely aroused body stole her breath.

Feeling a little nervous now, she circled her lips with the tip of her tongue in an unknowingly provocative gesture and blurted out, 'Oh, heavens.'

Drago gave a ragged laugh. '*Cara*, if you continue to look at me like you are doing I think I'll explode.' His voice thickened. 'It has to be now, *mia bella*. I can't wait any longer.'

As he knelt above her, his dark eyes glittering with the intensity of his desire, Jess's heart rate quickened and the slight fear she'd felt that he was too big and powerful for her to cope with faded. She had never been so aroused, so *desperate* to ease the aching need that throbbed in every pore of her body.

His skin felt warm beneath her palms as she

slid her hands over his chest and felt the faint abrasion of his chest hair. She loved the feeling of closeness to another human being. It was something she had rarely experienced. She did not remember her father ever hugging her as a child, and at the children's home the staff had been kind but never affectionate.

All Drago was offering was sex, she reminded herself. And that was all she wanted too—the satiation of this feverish yearning that blotted out all other thoughts and left her mindless with desire. Her heart thudded when he pulled her knickers down her legs and pushed her thighs apart. The deliberation of his actions increased her excitement and she whimpered when he touched her intimately again, the sensations he aroused as he found the most sensitive part of her making her arch her hips in urgent invitation.

The solid ridge of his erection jabbed her belly, but when she curled her fingers around his swollen manhood he made a harsh sound.

'Not this time, *cara*,' he growled as he pressed forward and entered her with a deep thrust that drove the breath from her lungs. Feeling her sudden tension, he stilled and stared into her eyes, a look of puzzlement in his. 'Did I hurt you?' His voice was rough with concern. 'I did not expect you to be so tight.'

She flushed. 'It's been a while,' she admitted, suddenly fearful that he would be disappointed by her.

'If it is uncomfortable for you we'll stop.'

'No!' Feeling him begin to withdraw, she clutched hold of him and wrapped her legs around his hips. 'I don't want to stop.'

Drago closed his eyes, struggling for control as his body reacted to the mind-blowing delight of feeling her vaginal muscles grip him in a velvet embrace. As Jess slowly relaxed he could not resist sinking deeper into her, and his buttocks clenched as he fought against the hot tide of pleasure that was threatening to overwhelm him.

'I'm not going to stop,' he assured her as he withdrew a little and she made a husky protest. If he was honest he did not think he *could* stop when his body was so tight and hot and hard, he acknowledged ruefully. 'See?' He thrust into her again—once, twice—each stroke harder and faster than the last as he set a rhythm that drove them both higher.

'Oh…' Jess gasped as he slid his hands beneath her bottom and tilted her so that the tip of his steel-hard arousal hit an especially sensitive spot deep within her. Waves of pleasure ripped through her as he plunged between her trembling thighs with an urgency that told her his control was close to breaking. Her breath came in short, sharp gasps, and she gripped the silk sheet beneath her, her fingers clawing at it as her excitement built to an intolerable level.

Nothing had prepared her for the ecstasy of her first ever orgasm. It overwhelmed her. Shock waves of incredible sensation pounded her and she shuddered with convulsive pleasure. Almost simultaneously she felt a tremor run through Drago's big body and he gave a harsh groan. The sound of it was somehow more shocking than anything that had gone before. The fact that this powerful man had come apart in her arms filled Jess with fierce tenderness, so that she curled her arms around his neck and stroked his hair as he laid his head on her breasts.

In the lull after the storm only the sound of their breathing gradually slowing broke the intense quiet, and in those moments when they were still joined it seemed to Jess that they were the only two people in a private, magical world.

Early next morning—so early that the light filtering through the crack in the curtains was a pale, iridescent glimmer—Jess lay still, pretending to be asleep, although in fact she was studying Drago from beneath her lashes.

He was lying on his back, staring up at the drapes of the four-poster bed. His hard-as-granite profile was not encouraging and her heart sank. Of course she had not expected to wake in his arms, or for him to kiss her tenderly as the new day dawned. She was stupid—falling into his bed last night had proved that—but she harboured no illusions that the passion they'd shared had been anything more than mind-blowing sex.

So why were tears blurring her vision? Why was she wishing with all her heart that he would pull her close and stroke her hair? She had been starved of affection all her life, so why did his indifference hurt so much?

Perhaps he sensed that she was awake, because he turned his head on the pillows. She blinked hard to dispel her tears. Pride was her faithful ally. No way was she going to act like a whipped puppy.

'Before you say anything, I'd like to agree. Last night was a mistake that should not have happened,' she said quickly. 'And it would definitely be best to forget about it.'

He frowned. 'How can you agree with me when I haven't made a comment? Can you read my mind?'

'I don't need to. You look…' Her heart lurched as she stared at his face. He looked gorgeous and incredibly sexy, with his silky hair falling onto his brow and dark stubble shading his jaw. She could not prevent the slight catch in her voice as she muttered, 'You look angry.'

Drago gave her a quizzical look. 'Well, it's true that I am angry—with myself. And I admit I *did* make a mistake last night. But I don't regret what happened between us and I definitely won't forget making love to you any time soon.'

The sultry gleam in his eyes sent a quiver of response through Jess. 'Then what mistake did you make?' she asked uncertainly.

'I forgot to use a condom.' His jaw tightened. 'I have no excuse other than that you have such an effect on me that I temporarily lost my sanity. I wanted you so badly I simply didn't think about protection. It was crass and irresponsible of me, and I apologise. I also want to assure you that I am healthy. I don't make a habit of having unprotected sex,' he said roughly.

Drago's self-respect had taken a hard knock when he had realised how stupid he had been. He had broken one of his golden rules. *Dio*, after what had happened with Vittoria he had always been so careful to avoid an unplanned pregnancy. He hoped that Jess took care of herself and used some method of contraception, but the knowledge that he had failed to act responsibly was a matter of bitter regret.

His frown deepened when he noticed how pale she looked this morning. In contrast to her white cheeks her lips were reddened and slightly swollen, and the faint bruises on her shoulders were shameful evidence that in his impatience to make love to her the previous night his touch had been too rough.

Guilt roughened his voice. 'I trust you will inform me if there are any consequences?'

'There won't be any,' Jess said in a quick, sharp voice.

She was painfully aware that her reply was based on wishful thinking rather than certainty. Her heart hammered against her ribs as the enormity of what she had done sank in, and she jerked upright, belatedly realising that she was naked. It was a bit late to feel self-conscious after she had spent a night of wild passion with Drago, she thought ruefully. But she could feel his gaze lingering on her breasts and she hastily pulled the sheet around her, wincing as the silk grazed nipples that felt ultra-sensitive from where he had kissed and sucked them.

She closed her eyes as memories of having sex with him flooded her mind. Not only had she behaved shamelessly, but she had been criminally stupid to forget about contraception. Dear heaven, how could she have taken such a risk again, when she had bitter experience of the consequences of having unprotected sex? Surely history would not repeat itself? Some women tried for years to fall pregnant. The odds of it happening to her again as a result of this one night must be a million to one, she tried to reassure herself.

Drago relaxed a little when he realised that Jess must be protected. She had sounded absolutely sure there was no risk she could have conceived. It did not change the fact that he was a damned fool, though. He could not believe he had allowed his desire for her to override his common sense. Even more disturbing was the fact that he was still not thinking logically. His mind was enjoying an erotic image of pushing her back against the pillows and tugging the sheet away from her body. Impossibly, he was even more turned on than he had been last night.

But she was sitting stiffly, hugging her knees, and her tension was palpable. He wondered if she regretted sleeping with him. She had been eager enough at the time, and afterwards she had curled up against him and fallen asleep almost instantly. God knew what she had dreamed about that had caused her to cry out in her sleep, he thought, frowning as he recalled the harrowing sobs that had racked her slender frame.

'Who is Daniel?' he asked abruptly. 'You called out the name during the night and you seemed to be upset,' he explained when she stared at him.

She bit her lip. 'He was a friend...my best friend. We grew up together in the children's home.' Her voice grew husky. 'He died when he was sixteen. He was hit by a car and suffered a serious head injury. He was on life support...but he never regained consciousness.'

Instinctively Drago reached for her hand and gave it a gentle squeeze. 'I'm sorry,' he said gruffly.

'I suppose seeing Angelo in the hospital brought back memories of the last time I saw Daniel. He looked like he was asleep and I kept thinking he would wake up.' Her throat moved as she swallowed hard. 'But the nurse said there was no hope. I'm so relieved that Angelo has regained consciousness.'

The raw emotion in her voice tugged on Drago's insides. Jess had known more than her fair share of pain in her young life, he thought heavily. He understood now why she had looked so pale when she had walked into the intensive care unit and seen Angelo in a coma. He felt guilty that he had not been more understanding, but he had not known about her past. He knew very little about her, he acknowledged, merely the small pieces presented to him by his private investigator.

Infuriated that he could not think straight when she was so close to him, and his senses were inflamed by the scent of her, he threw back the sheet and got out of bed. Making love to her last night had been an aberration he was determined not to repeat. Pulling on his robe, he headed for the bathroom, but paused in the doorway and glanced back at her.

'I have to go to the office this morning. Fico will take you to visit Angelo and I'll meet you at the hospital later.' He hesitated, still troubled by the memory of her distress during the night. 'You called out another name in your sleep. Was Katie also a friend from the children's home?'

A haunted expression flared in her eyes. 'Katie? I...I don't know anyone with that name. I've no idea what I was dreaming about.'

Drago stared at her for a few moments, noting how she avoided meeting his gaze. Why was she lying? he wondered as he closed the bathroom door and stepped into the shower. He felt frustrated that he knew so little about her. Jess's strange reaction was another puzzle to add to the intrigue surrounding her.

CHAPTER SEVEN

'SIX WEEKS WITH my leg in traction,' Angelo groaned. 'I think I'll go mad. If only my memory would come back. I feel as though my brain is surrounded by a grey mist.' He stared frustratedly at Jess, who was sitting beside his bed, helping herself to grapes from the fruit bowl. 'I don't understand why I was living in London and not Venice.'

'Drago said you had enrolled at a college to study business. Do you remember being at college?'

'No. And although you've told me I worked for your decorating company I have no recollection of it.' He frowned. 'To be honest, painting walls is not something I can imagine myself doing. Was I good at it?'

'Not very,' Jess admitted with a grimace.

'In that case why did you employ me?'

'You told me you were destitute and I wanted to help you.'

Angelo shook his head, as if the action would clear the fog from his mind. 'I lived with you, didn't I? In a big house surrounded by lots of trees? You cooked omelettes for dinner.'

Jess felt a flicker of excitement. 'You stayed at my flat for a few weeks. I made dinner for us the night before you disappeared. Can you remember where you were going, or why?'

'I'm sure it had something to do with Drago, but I just don't know what.'

'It's all right. Your memory will come back soon.' Jess squeezed Angelo's hand reassuringly. She hesitated for a moment. 'I suppose you don't remember why you withdrew a huge sum of money from your bank account, or who you gave it to?'

His brow furrowed. 'Money?'

'Yes, your inheritance fund—' Jess broke off when a noise from behind her alerted her to the fact that someone had entered the private hospital room.

'I'm sure Angelo will remember everything in

good time,' Drago said smoothly as he walked towards the bed.

He smiled at his cousin, but Jess sensed his anger, and when he glanced at her his black eyes were as hard as jet.

'I think you should get some rest now.' He spoke gently to Angelo. 'The nurse tells me you have been playing your guitar?'

'It's strange that I can remember some things.' Angelo sighed. 'Why do I get the feeling that there is some mystery surrounding me? Something that I was going to tell you just before the accident?'

'Try to relax. Jess has been here with you all day and I'm afraid she has overtired you.'

Bristling, Jess followed Drago out of the room. 'Thanks a lot,' she snapped as soon as he had closed the door. 'I didn't overtire him. He slept on and off during the day. I stayed because you said that talking to him might trigger his memory.'

'Perhaps you have another motive?' he said darkly. 'I don't want you to mention Angelo's missing inheritance fund in case you put ideas into his head.'

Nonplussed, she stared at him—and then wished she hadn't when she felt a coiling sensation in the pit of her stomach. Dressed in a pale grey suit teamed with a navy blue shirt, he looked incredibly sexy, and she could not help remembering him last night, naked and aroused as he had positioned himself over her.

'What sort of ideas?' she mumbled, thankful that he did not know what ideas were in *her* mind.

'Ideas such as he didn't give you a fortune. He's in a vulnerable state at the moment, and likely to believe anything you tell him.'

Drago's arrogant expression ignited Jess's temper like a flame set to tinder.

'For the last blasted time—I know nothing about Angelo's missing money,' she hissed.

She felt unbelievably hurt that although he had slept with her he clearly did not trust her. What had she expected? she asked herself miserably. He regarded her as good enough to have sex with but he did not respect her, and by falling into his bed so wantonly she had lost respect for herself.

'Where are you going?' he demanded.

'Anywhere so long as it's a long way away from

you.' She marched along the corridor without having a clue where she was heading.

'The exit is in the other direction.' Drago caught hold of her arm and swung her round to face him, feeling a stab of guilt when he saw tears shimmering in her eyes. 'I've had a difficult day,' he owned gruffly. 'I appreciate that you've given up a whole day to spend it with Angelo. Shall we go back to the *palazzo*…?'

'You mean you're giving me a *choice* of whether or not to return to my prison?' she said sarcastically.

'Madonna!' He raked a hand through his hair and glared at her in exasperation. 'You would test the patience of a saint. If you hate my home so much we'll go to a restaurant and get something to eat. Who knows? Perhaps a good meal will improve your temper.'

The restaurant was not scarily sophisticated, as Jess had feared, but a charming little place tucked away down a side street with tables set out on the terrace overlooking a narrow canal. The waiters were quietly attentive and seemed to know Drago.

'Trattoria Marisa is the place I come to when I want to chill out,' he admitted. He did not reveal that he never brought the women he dated here. In truth he did not know why he had brought Jess to the restaurant which he regarded as a sanctuary away from the stresses of his hectic life.

'What did the waiter say to you?' she asked curiously. 'And why did he keep looking at me?'

'He said that you are very beautiful and I am very lucky,' he said drily. He met her startled gaze and his mouth curved into a sudden smile. 'I agreed with him. You look stunning in that dress.'

Flustered, Jess glanced down at the white silk dress covered with a pattern of pink roses. Like all the clothes from the Cassa di Cassari collection it was pretty and elegant and made her feel very feminine. She studied the menu, which was in Italian and could have been written in hieroglyphics for all the sense it made.

'You had better order for me,' she murmured, and was even more disconcerted when Drago moved his chair closer to hers and patiently translated the choice of dishes. She found it hard to concentrate on what he was saying when she was achingly aware of the sensual musk of his aftershave. Her eyes seemed to have a magnetic attraction to his mouth. If he turned his head their lips would almost touch.

Her breath caught in her throat as he trapped her gaze, and she felt his warm breath feather across her lips. *Kiss me*, she willed him. She wanted him to so badly that she trembled, and her disappointment when he drew his head back from her felt like a knife through her heart.

His eyes darkened, and he gave a ragged laugh as he moved his chair back around the table. 'Sexual frustration is hell, isn't it, *mia bella*? You are driving me insane.'

Thankfully the waiter returned with the wine list and Jess did not have to reply.

The food served at Trattoria Marisa had been excellent as always, Drago mused later as he sipped his coffee. He had declined dessert but Jess had opted for an exotic concoction of chocolate ice-cream and whipped cream, which she had eaten with undisguised enjoyment. Had she any idea how much he was turned on by seeing the tip of her pink tongue lick the last morsel of cream from her spoon? he wondered with wry self-derision.

'Explain how you were set up to be accused of fraud,' he said abruptly.

Jess stiffened and gave him a rueful glance. 'I don't suppose you'll believe me.'

'Try me.'

She sighed. 'In a way I suppose it started with Daniel dying. He was the closest thing I had to a brother and I missed him terribly. I had to leave the children's home when I was sixteen. My social worker helped me find a bedsit and I got a job as a waitress in a café.'

She watched a gondola glide along the canal, her expression unknowingly wistful.

'I was lonely and grieving for Daniel. The highlight of my day was when a handsome businessman would come in to the café for his regular coffee. He would chat to me and ask me how I was, and he sounded as though he really cared.

His name was Sebastian Loxley. He told me he had just set up an internet company selling tickets for pop concerts and festivals, and he needed someone to work in the office. I couldn't believe it when he offered me the job. I was such a naïve fool,' Jess said bitterly. 'Seb must have found it so amusing to seduce me. I fell desperately in love with him, and when he invited me out to dinner on my seventeenth birthday and then took me back to his flat—well, let's just say he didn't have to try very hard to get me into his bed.'

'*Santa Madre!* You were a child,' Drago said harshly.

She shrugged. 'Not in legal terms. Unfortunately the law does little to protect vulnerable young adults. At my new job I faithfully followed the instructions I was given by Seb. Every time I took a credit card payment I made a separate record of the card details, including the security code, and passed the information on to Seb's accountant because apparently it was needed for tax purposes. I didn't question what I was doing.'

She blushed with embarrassment.

'I was bullied at school, so I didn't go very

often, and I left without any qualifications. I didn't understand about credit cards, and I had no idea that Marcus, the so-called accountant, ran an illegal business cloning cards, or that he paid Seb for the information I was passing to him. Eventually the police discovered the cloning scam, but Marcus must have had a tip-off and he disappeared abroad before they could arrest him. The trail led back to Seb's company and to me.'

Drago swore beneath his breath. 'Go on,' he encouraged when Jess hesitated.

'I was stunned when Seb told the police he was unaware of what I had been doing. I thought he would explain that he had instructed me to pass on the card details, but instead he put all the blame on me. The police believed him and decided that I had been working with Marcus. I was arrested. At the trial, Seb gave evidence against me.' Her voice shook. 'I thought he loved me. He'd even said we'd get married one day. But it was all lies. He didn't care about me. He didn't even want…'

'He didn't want what?' Drago prompted. He felt a curious pain in his gut when he saw the misery in her eyes. The feisty Jess he had come to know looked crushed. The idea that she had been preyed on by an unscrupulous crook when she had been so young filled him with rage, and a longing to smash his fist into Sebastian Loxley's face.

Jess shook her head. 'It doesn't matter,' she said dully. Seb's scathing response when she had told him she was pregnant with his baby was too painful to talk about. She glanced at Drago, searching for some sign that he believed her story, but his hard features were unreadable.

'What happened after the court case?'

'I felt I had hit rock-bottom,' she said huskily. 'I had no job, nowhere to live, and no self-respect. I met my social worker from the children's home, and she arranged for me to stay with a couple who'd had experience fostering troubled teenagers.' A soft smile lit her face. 'Ted and Margaret were wonderful people. It's no exaggeration to say that they changed my life. For the first time ever I felt part of a family. Ted ran a decorating business and he took me on as an apprentice. I discovered a natural talent for woodwork, and I went to college and trained in carpentry before Ted took me on as a business partner. The T and J in the company name stands for Ted and Jess.'

Jess broke off as a waiter came up to the table to offer them more coffee. The interruption gave Drago the opportunity to mull over everything she had told him. He did not even question whether he believed her story. The emotion in her voice when she had spoken of how she had been so cruelly betrayed by the man she had loved had been too raw to be an act. But the question of whether or not he trusted her still remained. Until his cousin's memory returned there was no possibility of discovering if Jess knew what had happened to Angelo's missing inheritance fund, Drago acknowledged frustratedly.

As they were about to leave the restaurant a gondola drew up alongside the terrace. Like most Venetians, Drago was unimpressed by a mode of transport used almost exclusively by tourists, but after catching the hopeful look in Jess's eyes he called to the gondolier to assist her into the boat.

Dusk was falling, and the sun was a fiery orb sinking below the horizon, streaking the sky with gold and pink and casting golden shadows on the elegant buildings which lined the canal.

'It's so beautiful,' Jess breathed.

It was also incredibly romantic, sitting beside Drago in the gondola, but it was doubtful he thought so, she acknowledged ruefully. He had given no indication that he believed she had unwittingly been involved in the fraud scam when she had worked for Seb. She wondered why she cared about his opinion of her. She wasn't dishonest, and when Angelo regained his memory he would explain what he had done with his inheritance fund and Drago would realise he had misjudged her. But what if Angelo never recovered from his amnesia? she thought anxiously. The truth about his missing money might never be uncovered and Drago would always think the worst of her.

He could not force her to stay in Venice for ever, she reminded herself. But in order to return to England she would first have to organise a new passport, and to do that she needed her bank card, which was also in her rucksack at the bottom of the canal. Everything seemed complicated, and sleeping with Drago last night had confused the situation even more. She must have been mad. It was no excuse that her common sense had been obliterated by the firestorm of passion that had ignited between her and Drago. No excuse at all…

She darted him a glance, and her heart missed a beat when her eyes met his brooding gaze. The evening air was cool, and he frowned when he saw her shiver.

'Here—take this,' he said as he slipped off his jacket and draped it around her shoulders.

'Thank you.' Was that breathy, seductive whisper really her voice?

The silk lining of the jacket retained the warmth of his body and felt sensuous against her bare arms. She wished it was his arms around her rather than the jacket, and recalled with shocking clarity how wonderful his naked body had felt when he had pulled her beneath him and made love to her. Desperate to banish her traitorous thoughts, she closed her eyes. But images remained of Drago's bronzed chest, overlaid with the whorls of dark hair that had scraped the sensitive tips of her breasts when he had lowered himself onto her.

'I still want you, too,' his deep, gravelly voice whispered in her ear, and his breath feathered her cheek. Her lashes flew open and, startled, she caught her breath when she saw the hunger in his eyes that glittered like polished jet.

'I don't…'

'Yes, *cara*, you do.' He captured her denial with his lips and banished it with a kiss that was fiercely passionate yet held an underlying gentleness that was unexpected and utterly beguiling.

Jess lost her battle with herself. The pleasure of having Drago's mouth move over hers was impossible to resist, and when he traced his tongue over the tight line of her clamped lips she gave a little moan and parted them so that the kiss became intensely erotic.

Lost in the magic he was creating, Jess stared at him helplessly when at last he lifted his head. 'If it's any consolation, I don't know what the hell is going on either,' he told her roughly. 'This was not meant to happen.'

Drago's taut voice revealed his frustration. He

disliked public displays of affection and could not believe that he had kissed Jess on a gondola in the middle of Venice's main waterway. At least the gondolier had discreetly averted his gaze, and when they drew up by the Palazzo d'Inverno he handed the man a large tip.

Jess walked ahead of Drago into the *palazzo*, her stiletto heels tapping on the marble floor, echoing the staccato beat of her heart.

He caught up with her as she reached the stairs. 'What would you like to do for the rest of the evening? I have a selection of English DVDs if you want to watch a film.'

She tore her eyes from the sensual curve of his mouth that only a few moments ago had decimated her ability to think, and knew that she dared not spend another minute alone with him. 'If you don't mind, I'd like to go straight to bed.'

His sudden grin stole her breath. Without his usual arrogant expression he looked almost boyish and heart-stoppingly sexy.

'Excellent idea,' he murmured.

She flushed with mortification when she realised he had taken her words as an invitation, but her frantic, 'I meant *alone*,' was muffled against his shoulder as he scooped her into his arms and strode up the stairs. 'Drago—we can't,' she whispered when he reached his suite of rooms and carried her through to the bedroom. 'Last night was a mistake.'

He tumbled her onto the bed and came down on top of her so that she felt the hard proof of his arousal nudge her thigh. Threading his fingers through her hair, he stared into her eyes, the amusement fading from his.

'Last night was inevitable from the moment we met,' he said harshly.

It was the truth. She had taken one look at him and fallen in lust—not love, Jess quickly assured herself. No way would she risk her heart with *him*. But no other man had ever made her feel this way. He kissed her mouth, her cheeks, her eyelids—light, delicate kisses that melted the last vestiges of her resistance. His fingers tugged open the buttons running down the front of her dress and he gave a low murmur of approval when he pushed the material aside and discovered that she was not wearing a bra.

'Bellisima,' he said thickly as he cupped her small breasts in his hands and anointed one dusky peak and then the other with his lips.

She caught fire, arching her slender body to meet his mouth and eagerly helping him to remove her dress and knickers. This was not the time for words; their need was too urgent. Drago stripped with a clumsy haste that was strangely touching, and after taking a condom from the bedside drawer and sliding it over the proud jut of his arousal he moved over her.

Jess caught her breath as he entered her. He filled her, completed her, and she wrapped her legs around him and held on tightly to his shoulders as he possessed her with deep, measured strokes, driving her higher. As her body trembled with the exquisite ripples of orgasm her heart soared, and when Drago groaned with the power of his own release she felt a fierce tenderness and the strangest sense that their souls had joined.

The crowds of tourists in St Mark's Square had thinned in the early evening and the restaurants became busier. Sitting beneath the striped awning of a café on the edge of the square, her elbow propped on the table and her hand cupping her chin, Jess had a clear view of the ornate and incredibly beautiful Basilica.

'I think I'm in love,' she murmured. Beside her she felt Drago stiffen, and when she glanced at him and saw his startled frown she laughed. 'Not with you. With Venice.'

'Ah.' His relief was evident in his smile.

For some reason Jess felt a little pang of regret that he wanted nothing more from her than sex. *Don't be an idiot,* she told herself sternly. She knew their affair was based purely on their physical attraction to one another. Their sex-life was amazing, but inevitably the fiery passion they shared would burn out.

'At the weekend we can climb to the top of the Campanile again, if you like,' he offered. 'I know how much you enjoyed the views over the city. Or I'll take you to see the Doge's Palace. The interior is impressive, and filled with stunning artworks. And of course you can't visit Venice without walking over the Bridge of Sighs.'

'It's such a romantic name. I wonder why it's called that?'

'The popular explanation is rather less romantic than the name suggests. The bridge used to lead to the state prison, and crossing it would often be a prisoner's last view of Venice.'

Jess sighed. 'I feel guilty sightseeing when Angelo is stuck in hospital.'

'You have visited him every day for the past few weeks, and I know how much he appreciates your company. Angelo would not begrudge you some free time,' Drago insisted.

'But I shouldn't have free time. I should be at home, running my business.' Jess chewed her bottom lip with her teeth—something she unconsciously did when she was anxious. 'I know that when I phoned Mike he said everything is fine, and that he had secured a new contract for T&J Decorators to refurbish a commercial property, but I need to go back and take charge. My company means everything to me. It's the only thing I've ever succeeded at,' she admitted ruefully.

'Once Angelo's memory has returned you will be free to leave.'

Drago's smile was full of easy charm but his tone was uncompromising, and Jess's spirits plummeted with the realisation that he still suspected she had some involvement with his cousin's missing inheritance fund. And in truth she *was* still his prisoner, for she never went anywhere without either him or his bodyguard Fico to accompany her. On a couple of occasions during the first week of her stay she had attempted to slip away from the bodyguard. It had crossed her mind that if she explained her situation to one of the nurses at the hospital they might help her. But none that she had met spoke English, Fico had followed her doggedly, and she still had the problem of no passport or money.

Jess pushed away the uncomfortable thought that she had not tried harder to leave Venice because she was captivated by her affair with Drago. His hunger for her showed no sign of abating. But aside from their mutual desire for one another a sense of companionship, even friendship, had unexpectedly developed between them. He had given her several guided tours of Venice, and Jess loved wandering around the city with him, exploring the narrow streets and the many charming *piazzas*. She visited Angelo every day while Drago was at work. Usually he met her at the hospital in the evening, and after spending some time with his cousin they would return to the *palazzo* or go for dinner at a restaurant—the Trattoria Marisa being their favourite place to eat.

'How was Angelo today?'

'He still has a bad headache.' She frowned as her thoughts returned to Angelo. 'It has lasted for three days now, and your aunt is very concerned.'

Dorotea had admitted as much. After spending endless days cooped up with her in the small hospital room Angelo's mother had thawed slightly towards Jess, and had even thanked her for her efforts to help her son. Drago's mother was also friendlier, but once or twice Jess had been aware of Luisa's speculative glance, and she had a feeling that Luisa knew she was sleeping with her son.

'I'll speak to the consultant about him—' Drago broke off and smiled at a small child who had toddled over from where his parents were sitting at a nearby table.

The little boy was about two years old, Jess

estimated, and utterly adorable, with a halo of blond curls and big blue eyes. He seemed to be intrigued by Drago, and grinned as he waved the sticky ice-cream cone he was holding.

'*No*, Josh!' The child's mother hurried over just as the toddler smeared ice-cream over Drago's superbly tailored trousers. 'I'm so sorry...' she said in English.

Drago interrupted her frantic apology with a laugh. 'Don't worry. He's an angelic-looking child,' he said, in a soft tone that captured Jess's attention.

'He can be a little terror,' the woman said ruefully. She glanced at Jess. 'You know what they're like at two—into everything.'

She nodded at the woman and smiled back, trying to ignore the knife-blade that sliced through her heart. What had Katie been like at two years old? she wondered. Had she been 'into everything'? She would never know, and the reminder of all she had lost was an ache inside her that never went away.

The woman picked up the little boy and carried him back to her table. 'Cute kid,' Drago commented as he attempted to clean his trousers with a napkin.

'I've noticed that Italians really seem to love children,' Jess said musingly. 'Have you never wanted to marry and have children?'

'I'm happy with my life the way it is.'

Puzzled by the sudden curtness in his voice, Jess studied him curiously. 'You were so gentle with that little boy. I think you would make a great father.'

'*Madonna!* Can we drop the subject?' he snapped. 'My personal life is not up for discussion.'

Jess felt a flare of irritation at his arrogant tone. 'Why not?' she demanded. 'I've told you things about me and what happened with Seb. Why don't you want to talk about yourself?'

He made no response, and the hard gleam in his eyes warned her to back off, but Jess refused to be dismissed. She knew she meant nothing to Drago, but the reminder that he only wanted a sexual relationship with her hurt more than it should.

'Maybe you're hiding some terrible secret?' she taunted.

'Don't be ridiculous.'

His mouth tightened, and to Jess's surprise he seemed uncomfortable. She sensed there was something in his past that he wanted to keep hidden. Was it a woman? He had a reputation as a playboy, but perhaps he'd once had a relationship that had been important to him. The idea evoked a sharp stab of jealousy inside her.

'Have you ever been in love?' she blurted out.

His eyes narrowed and his impatience was tangible, but after a few moments he shrugged and admitted tautly, 'Once. A long time ago.'

Jess caught her breath. 'What happened?'

'Nothing happened. The relationship ended and I grew up. It was an educational experience,' he said, with heavy irony that made Jess even more intrigued. It sounded as though he had been hurt, and she guessed he had not wanted his relationship with the woman he had loved to end. She longed to ask him more questions, but he did not give her the opportunity as he glanced at his watch and stood up.

'I'm going to the hospital to talk to the doctor about Angelo's headaches,' he said abruptly. 'Fico will take you back to the *palazzo*. The party is due to start at eight o'clock tonight.' He made an effort to lighten his tone. 'I'm sure you will want to spend some time getting ready. I appreciate that you have agreed to act as my hostess. This dinner party is an annual event attended by senior management staff from Cassa di Cassari's worldwide operation. My mother and aunt usually attend, but this year they naturally wish to devote their time to Angelo.'

'No problem,' Jess said in a fiercely bright voice.

She was determined not to let him see how hurt she felt by his refusal to talk about himself, and equally determined to hide the fact that she was feeling nervous about her role as hostess at the party. Drago had assured her that most of the guests would be able to speak English, but what on earth did a decorator have in common with high-flying businessmen and company executives from the world famous Cassa di Cassari? she thought anxiously.

As she stood up she was overcome by an unpleasant sensation that the pavement beneath her feet was tilting, and she gripped the edge of the table.

'What's the matter?' Drago asked, frowning as he watched the rosy pink flush on her cheeks fade so that she looked ashen.

'I just feel a bit dizzy. It'll pass in a minute.'

He looked unconvinced. 'I hope you're not coming down with something. You felt dizzy when you got up this morning.'

'It's nothing.' Jess dismissed his concern, not revealing that she had waited until he had left for work before she had rushed to the bathroom to be sick the last two mornings. 'Maybe I've had too much sun. It's much hotter here in Venice than in London, and I'm not used to the heat.' That had to be the explanation, she assured herself.

'With your delicate colouring you need to wear a hat.' Drago smoothed a tendril of her fiery gold hair back from her face and could not resist dropping a light kiss on her soft mouth. 'I adore your freckles, *cara*. Especially the ones that look like gold-dust scattered over your breasts,' he murmured, his voice dropping to a sexy whisper that sent a little shiver of response down Jess's spine.

One look from his glittering black gaze was all it took to make her melt, she acknowledged wryly. As she picked up her bag the magazine she had bought at the hospital slid out and fell on the floor. Drago bent to pick it up, but instead of handing it to her he stared at the front cover and his expression darkened.

'Why do you read such trash? Gossip magazines print utter rubbish,' he said tersely, flicking through the pages with a look of arrogant disdain on his face that irked Jess.

'I suppose you think I should only read highbrow novels by classical authors such as...' She frantically searched her mind for an author she had heard of whom he would deem suitable. 'Dickens.' It was the only name she could come up with. 'Actually, I bought that magazine because it mainly has photos of celebrities' houses, and I'm interested in interior design. I can't read it because I don't understand Italian. But don't think that I read literary stuff at home, because I don't. Unlike you, I wasn't born into a wealthy family and I don't have the advantage of a good education.'

Jess could not hide the tremor in her voice. Drago was highly intelligent and had an extensive knowledge of many subjects. She felt embarrassed by her lack of education, and he clearly thought she was a brainless bimbo. 'At least I'm not a snob, who criticises other people for their tastes,' she finished hotly.

Drago raked a hand through his hair. 'I wasn't trying to insult you. *Dio*, you are such a firebrand.'

His exasperation faded and he felt an unexpected tug of tenderness when he saw the glimmer of tears in her eyes. He was unwilling to explain that the photograph of a beautiful socialite on the front cover of the magazine was an unwelcome reminder of his past. Nor could he explain to Jess that watching the little boy in the café had evoked an ache in his gut. Some things were best left buried. He had never before felt inclined to talk about his past to any of his lovers, and there was no reason why he should do so with Jess, he told himself.

He gave a frustrated sigh when he saw Fico's burly figure heading towards them across the square. What he wanted to do was take Jess back to the *palazzo* and make love to her but, as always, duty to his family prevailed. He was concerned about his cousin, and had promised his aunt that he would speak to the consultant and find out whether Angelo's headaches were an indication of something more serious.

CHAPTER EIGHT

WHERE WAS DRAGO? Jess glanced at the clock for the hundredth time, and her tension escalated when she saw that it was ten to eight. Any minute now the party guests would begin to arrive, expecting to be greeted by their host. Instead they would be met by a hostess whose social skills were sadly inadequate, she thought, feeling another stab of nervousness at the prospect of the evening ahead. Fortunately Drago's butler Francesco was his usual unflappable self, and had informed her that the household staff had completed all the preparations for the party.

Leaving her bedroom, which she had never actually slept in during her stay at the *palazzo* but used as a dressing room, she walked back to the master suite and felt weak with relief when Drago strolled into the sitting room from his bedroom.

'There you are!' Her relief gave way to anger as

she watched him calmly adjust his cufflinks as if he had all the time in the world. 'Where have you been? I've been worried sick.'

His brows lifted. 'Why, *cara*, I didn't know you cared,' he drawled.

'I meant I was worried you wouldn't get back in time.' She fell silent, puzzled by his attitude, and by the strange feeling that he was avoiding her gaze. 'Were you delayed at the hospital? How is Angelo?'

'He's fine.' Perhaps realising that he had sounded curt, Drago finally looked at her. 'We'll talk about him later,' he said obliquely.

He smiled suddenly, and Jess felt a familiar knee-jerk reaction as he roamed his eyes over her.

His voice softened. 'You look amazing, *mia bella*. The dress is perfect for you.'

She flushed, feeling stupidly shy. 'It's a beautiful dress. I've never worn anything like it before.'

The full-length royal blue satin gown that Jess had discovered in her room when she had gone to change for the party was exquisite; the deceptively simple design flattered her slender figure and the crystal studded shoulder straps and narrow belt gave the dress extra glamour. One of the maids had helped her with her hair, and had swept it up into a sleek chignon. Three-inch sliver stiletto sandals gave her additional height, and when Jess had studied her reflection in the mirror she had been shocked to see herself looking so elegant.

'Is the dress from the Cassa di Cassari range of clothes?'

'No. I asked the designer Torre Umberto to make it especially for you. This will be a perfect accessory for the dress.'

As he walked towards her Drago took something from his pocket. Jess gasped when he held it up and she saw that it was a strand of glittering diamonds interspersed with square-cut sapphires.

'I don't think I should wear it. Supposing I lose it?' she said nervously. A little shiver ran through her when she felt his warm breath on the back of her neck as he fastened the necklace around her throat.

'Of course you won't lose it.' He turned her towards the mirror and she caught her breath at the sight of the diamonds sparkling with fiery brilliance against her skin.

'I feel like I've stepped into the pages of a fairy tale,' she whispered, staring at the reflection of the beautiful woman whom she hardly recognised as herself, and the dark, dangerously attractive man standing behind her. She gave another shiver when Drago bent his head and trailed his lips down the length of her slender white neck. In the mirror she watched his eyes glitter with a look she knew so well, and his hunger for her made her insides melt.

He turned her to face him, but instead of kissing her, as she longed for him to do, he stepped away from her and ran a hand through his hair.

'Jess…we need to talk.'

Puzzled that he seemed uncharacteristically ill at ease, she said quietly, 'What about?'

He cursed at the sound of a knock on the door, and strode across the room to open it. After a brief conversation with the butler he glanced back at her, his frustration that they had been interrupted revealed in his taut voice. 'Francesco says that some of the guests have arrived. We had better go down and greet them.'

Her foster-mother had had a habit of quoting proverbs, and one in particular—*You can't make a silk purse out of a sow's ear*—had never seemed more appropriate, Jess brooded later in the evening. Thanks to the *haute couture* dress she was wearing she did not look out of place among the glamorous women party guests. But it had quickly become apparent that she did not fit into Drago's rarefied world of the sophisticated super-rich.

Dinner had been a nightmare; she hadn't known which cutlery to use for each course, and she'd managed to knock over a glass of wine belonging to the guest sitting next to her. One of the waiters had calmly mopped up the mess, but she'd felt everyone's eyes on her and wanted to die of embarrassment.

The fact that she did not speak Italian had not proved a problem, as most of the guests spoke English, but while they'd discussed a range of subjects including politics, current affairs and the arts, Jess had struggled to find something to say. She knew nothing about opera, she had never skied in Aspen—or anywhere else for that matter—and enquiries about her chosen career were met with surprise followed by an awkward silence when she revealed that she ran a decorating company.

It would have been better if Drago had hosted the party on his own, she thought dismally. And from the way he had avoided her all evening it seemed he thought so too. While cocktails had been served he had mingled with his guests and hardly spoken a word to her. Now, during dinner, although he was sitting opposite her, he focused his attention on the two beautiful women seated on either side of him and paid her scant attention. As coffee and *petit-fours* were served he lapsed into a brooding silence, and his grim expression deterred anyone from approaching him.

'Of course I'm not surprised that our host looks so dour,' the woman sitting next to Jess commented in an undertone.

'What do you mean?' She cast a sideways glance towards the elegant wife of Drago's chief financial officer, who had introduced herself as Theresa Petronelli.

'I imagine any man would find it hard to see pictures of his ex-fiancée, her husband and two children looking the epitome of the perfect family on the front page of a top-selling magazine. It must be a kick in the teeth for Drago—and a painful reminder of what he lost.'

Shock ran though Jess. 'Are you saying he was once engaged to be married?'

'To the lovely Vittoria—who I have to say looks simply stunning in this week's edition of *Vita* magazine,' Theresa confirmed. 'Drago was engaged to her years ago, and Vittoria's parents' organised a lavish wedding. Then out of the blue the relationship ended. There were rumours that Vittoria was rushed into hospital, but no one from the family would say what was wrong with her, or whether her illness had anything to do with the ending of their relationship. The paparazzi hounded Drago for his side of the story but he remained tight-lipped about what had happened.

'I've often wondered if he was more upset by the split than he let on,' Theresa confided. 'Vittoria's father is a count. She is very beautiful and gracious, and would have been the perfect wife for Drago, but a couple of years ago she married a Swiss banker and she has just given birth to their second child.'

It was *Vita* magazine that had fallen out of her bag earlier, Jess thought. She hadn't understood why Drago had seemed in such a bad mood when he had flicked through the pages, but from what Theresa had said he had clearly been dismayed to see pictures of his ex-fiancée who was now happily married to someone else.

Presumably Vittoria was the woman he had once been in love with. Was he still in love with her? she wondered. For some strange reason the thought caused a sharp pain in her chest, as if she had been stabbed in the heart. Her eyes were drawn across the table to him, and she stiffened when she discovered that he was watching her with a curious intensity.

He leaned forward suddenly, his dark gaze trapping hers. 'Are you enjoying the party?'

Hurt by his indifference towards her all evening, she saw no reason why she should be tactful. 'Not really. I feel out of my depth among all these posh people. The kind of party I'm used to is a barbecue in the rain, burnt sausages and my team of workmen having a competition to see how much beer they can drink. I don't belong here.' She looked away from him, cursing the silly tears that stung her eyes as she added silently, *with you.*

Drago frowned. 'That's not true. Of course you belong here. You are my guest.'

'I'm your prisoner, suspected of something I have not done,' Jess said fiercely, thankful that Theresa Petronelli was chatting to another guest and not listening to her conversation with Drago.

He gave her a sardonic look. 'I'm sure that someone as resourceful as you could have left Italy if you had really wanted to. Which makes me think that perhaps you wanted to stay with me,' he drawled.

'Of course I wanted to leave,' she snapped, outraged by his suggestion. 'But thanks to you my passport is at the bottom of the canal.'

'Thanks to me? I had nothing to do with your crazy climb down from a second-floor balcony—

except to save you when you fell. You're kidding yourself, *cara*. You stayed because you love the way I make you feel,' he stated, in his deep, sexy voice that caressed her senses like crushed velvet.

She stared at him and felt her stomach dip. He looked incredibly handsome in a dinner suit and white silk shirt. The candles on the table cast a flickering light that accentuated the hard angles and planes of his chiselled features, and his dark hair had fallen onto his brow. Jess longed to run her fingers through it.

She'd stayed because she had fallen in love with him.

Jess swallowed as the shocking realisation hit her and quickly lowered her eyelashes, terrified that he might be able to read her thoughts. She cautiously examined the idea and gave a silent groan at her stupidity. Images flashed into her mind of walking hand in hand with him through the streets of Venice, of the candlelit dinners they'd had at Trattoria Marisa, where he was always able to relax after a hectic day at work and they'd talk about nothing in particular, in the way that lovers do. And underlying their easy companionship was the simmering sexual attraction which ignited the moment he took her in his arms and always culminated in him making love to her with hungry passion and an unexpected tenderness that somehow eased the loneliness inside her.

To her relief one of the guests stood up and proposed a toast to Cassa di Cassari's chairman. This apparently signified the end of the party, and Jess took advantage of the bustle of people getting up from the table and preparing to leave to slip upstairs. Out of habit she went straight to Drago's suite, but as she walked into his bedroom she stopped and stared at herself in the mirror. She looked lovely in the fairy-tale dress, but she didn't look like the Jess Harper who ran a decorating business and was more used to wearing painting overalls. It was time to end the madness. She had thought she could have an affair with Drago without her emotions getting involved, but now that she had committed the ultimate folly of falling for him she had to end her relationship with him.

The headache that had started earlier had developed into a thudding sensation in her skull and she felt nauseous again. Maybe she had picked up a virus and that was why she had felt sapped of energy for the last few days. Releasing her hair from the chignon lessened the pain in her head a little, and after running a brush through her hair she unfastened the diamond necklace, wondering where she should put it. It must be worth a fortune. She guessed Drago probably stored it in a safe, but for now she decided to slip it into his bedside drawer.

His passport was lying on top of some papers. She carefully placed the necklace in the drawer, her attention still on the passport—which, to her surprise, was an English one, not an Italian passport. Curiosity got the better of her. After a moment's hesitation she opened it—and a bolt of shock ran though her. It was impossible! Her passport had been in the rucksack that was now at the bottom of the canal. Staring at the photo of herself, she felt utterly confused.

The click of the door being closed made her swing round. Clutching the passport, she said helplessly, 'I don't understand. Why is my passport in your drawer?'

'I removed it from your bag when you first arrived at the *palazzo*.' Drago gave a laconic shrug. 'It seemed the best way to ensure you stayed in Italy until I was ready for you to leave.'

'But you know I've been worrying about how I can get a replacement.' Jess's temper ignited. 'How dare you deceive me?' She gave a bitter laugh. 'But why am I surprised? I should be used to men lying to me. You're just the same as Seb—devious and controlling...' Her voice cracked as the realisation of Drago's lack of trust in her sank in. How stupid she had been to believe that they had become friends as well as lovers while she had been in Venice. To her horror, she felt a tear slide down her cheek. Angrily she dashed it away. Pride was all she had, and she lifted her chin and glared at him. 'You have accused me unjustly and treated me unfairly. I know nothing about your cousin's missing money—'

She broke off as Drago strode across the room towards her, his eyes blazing with an expression she could not define.

'I *know*,' he said roughly. 'Angelo has regained his memory and he remembers everything. That's why I was delayed at the hospital.'

It was one shock too many. Jess sank down weakly onto the bed. 'You mean he remembers what he did with his inheritance fund? Why didn't you say something earlier instead of avoiding me at the party?' she demanded, unable to hide the tremor in her voice.

Drago exhaled slowly. He prided himself on his good judgement, and was rarely wrong, but he had been very wrong about Jess and had no idea how he was going to make amends for the way he had jumped to conclusions about her.

'I'm sorry,' he said roughly. 'I did not know what to say to you. I have so many things to apologise for that I don't know where to begin. 'Angelo invested his money in a gold mine,' he continued after a moment. 'It sounds crazy, I know,' he said when he saw the startled look on Jess's face. 'Apparently while he was at college in London he met some people who told him about an investment opportunity at a mine on the west coast of Australia. The owners had proof that there was a lot of gold underground, and were looking for investors to put up funds to start mining it. Angelo was convinced that the investment was sound, and was assured that once the mine was running he would triple his investment, so he went ahead without first discussing it with me.

'A few months later he discovered that he had been duped. The whole thing turned out to be a scam run by confidence tricksters. Instead of asking for my help, Angelo was so ashamed that he'd been fooled that he felt he couldn't come home. He *was* literally destitute, but thankfully you gave him a job and somewhere to live. He admits he dreaded telling me what he had done,' Drago said heavily. 'He says he felt I was too controlling, and he wanted to prove that he could succeed in business to impress me.' He grimaced. 'All these years I have taken care of him and tried to be a father figure to him. I had no idea he resented me.'

Jess heard the hurt in his voice and could not help but feel sympathetic. 'I'm sure he doesn't re-sent you,' she said softly. 'He just needs to find his own way in life.'

'He doesn't want a position in Cassa di Cassari. He wants to be a professional musician,' Drago muttered. 'I wish he'd told me about the investment scam. It would have saved a lot of trouble. When Aunt Dorotea revealed that she knew he had withdrawn all his money from the bank he panicked and told her he had lent it to an English friend—Jess Harper. Naturally my aunt was worried, and asked me to find out more about you.'

'And when you learned that I had been found guilty of fraud you believed I had somehow conned the money from Angelo,' Jess said dully. She stiffened as Drago sat down next to her on the bed. The musky scent of his aftershave teased her senses and she resented her fierce awareness of him. She felt ashamed that, even knowing he had a low opinion of her, she had fallen into his bed willingly.

Drago glanced at Jess's white face and his gut clenched with guilt at the way he had treated her. 'Eventually Angelo decided he had to own up to what he had done. But on his way here to see me he was involved in the car accident. I was instantly suspicious of you because I have had experience of being conned,' he explained grimly. 'When I was a similar age to Angelo I was thrust into the role of chairman of Cassa di Cassari, after my father and uncle died. I was young, and determined to prove myself a worthy successor to my father. I was impressed by an investment opportunity in Russia—although if I'm totally honest I was more impressed by the exotic and very beautiful Russian woman who persuaded me to put a huge amount of Cassa di Cassari's money into her company,' he admitted with wry self-derision. 'Natalia must have found it very amusing to seduce me, but when she disappeared with several million pounds of the company's money the board members were rather less than impressed.

'I cursed myself for being a gullible fool and worked like a dog to regain the board's support. I'd learned a valuable lesson and was more careful about who I trusted. I admit that discovering you had a criminal record made me suspicious of you. But when I met you at your flat—' He broke off and shook his head at the memory of their first meeting. 'You blew me away,' he said thickly. 'I took one look at you and was smitten. I felt violently jealous that you might be my cousin's lover. It was easy to believe that Angelo had been conned by a beautiful woman, as had once happened to me. But within a very short time I began to wonder if I had misjudged you. You were so kind to Angelo, and spent hours at the hospital trying to jog his memory. Rather than seeming worried about what he might remember, you were adamant that he would exonerate you—which he did, completely, when I visited him tonight.'

Looking into Jess's eyes, Drago said strongly, 'I believe the Loxley guy set you up, and that you are innocent of the crime you were convicted of. Soon after I brought you to the *palazzo* I started to have doubts that you knew anything about Angelo's missing money.' Catching her doubtful expression, he grimaced. 'I understand why you might not believe me.'

'You hid my passport,' she said sharply. 'Why would you have done that if you trusted me?'

He looked away from her and said, in a strangely muted voice, 'There was a reason why I wanted you to stay that had nothing to do with my cousin.'

Jess frowned; puzzled by his sudden tension evident in the rigid line of his jaw. 'What reason?'

Drago had asked himself the same question numerous times and still did not have a clear answer. He did not understand what his feelings were for Jess. All he knew was that he had never felt this way about any of his previous mistresses. He had tried to convince himself that his fascination with her was simply because they had great sex, but deep down he knew it was something more than that. He was not ready to examine his emotions, but now his hand had been forced—and if he did not want Jess to catch the next flight to London he knew he would have to lower his barriers.

He looked into her green eyes and saw her confusion. 'I didn't want to lose you,' he admitted quietly. 'I still don't.'

The huskiness in Drago's voice made Jess's heart flip. Was he saying that their relationship meant something to him? That *she* meant something to him?

She swallowed. 'I don't understand. Angelo's memory has returned, and you know I had nothing to do with his missing money.' She cast a rueful look at the passport in her hand. 'Why shouldn't I go home?'

'You know why, *cara*. You feel it too.'

It was the one thing Drago was sure of. This inexplicable thing that was happening to him, that made him think about her at inconvenient times and made him want to be with her all the time—he was certain that Jess felt the same way. He had seen evidence of it in the way her face lit up whenever she saw him, and in her sleepy, sexy smile when she woke in his arms every morning. She was so beautiful. Simply looking at her made his insides ache. He knew that if he touched her he wouldn't be able to stop, and his hand was unsteady as he threaded his fingers into her glorious autumn-gold hair and tilted her face to his.

'I have never desired any woman the way I desire you, *mia bella*.' He gently traced his thumb-pad over the curve of her lower lip. 'I would like our relationship to continue.'

Jess's heart was beating so fast that she was sure he must feel it when he placed his hand just below her breast. She was stunned by Drago's revelation that he did not want their affair to end yet. He had not promised commitment of any kind, she reminded herself, but the voice of caution inside her head was drowned out by the thunderous beat of her heart. Drago wanted her, and she did not care for how long.

Reality poked its nose into her fairy tale. How could she continue this affair with him when she needed to return to London to run her decorating business? She was sure that Drago would soon tire of a long-distance relationship. What if he suggested that she move to Venice? She would be a fool to give up her business for the sake of an affair with him that doubtless would end after a few months—yet the thought of leaving him and never seeing him again ripped her apart.

Jess's thoughts were reeling. She wanted to ask Drago what he meant when he said he wanted their relationship to continue, and how exactly their affair would work, but she was afraid of his reply. If he asked her to give up her life in London she was scared she might be tempted to agree.

Feeling too restless and worked up to remain sitting next to him, she jumped up from the bed. The room spun and she felt dizzy again—as she had after she'd ridden on a carousel years ago, when her social worker had taken her to a fairground. She felt hot and cold at the same time, there was a peculiar roaring noise in her ears, and she heard Drago calling her name as she fell into blackness.

CHAPTER NINE

THE ROOM WAS no longer spinning. Cautiously Jess turned her head and met Drago's tense gaze.

'Lie still. The doctor is on his way.'

She immediately jerked upright—and gagged as a wave of nausea swept over her.

'*Dio!* Do you ever do as you are told?' Concern overrode the impatience in his voice as he eased her back down onto the pillows.

'My dress will get creased if I lie down in it,' she argued, although she did not try to move again for the simple reason that she was afraid she would be sick. 'I don't need a doctor.'

His answer was uncompromising. 'Of course you do. You passed out, you're as white as death, and you've been suffering from dizzy spells.'

It was easier to let Drago take control, Jess decided wearily. And in truth she felt awful.

The doctor arrived a few minutes later. A softly

spoken man, with grey hair and a reassuringly calm manner, he checked her blood pressure, asked various questions and took a blood sample which he said he would test to see if she was anaemic.

'It is a fairly common problem with young women as iron is lost during menstruation each month—especially if they do not eat properly because of the fashion to be thin,' he said, with a meaningful glance at Jess's slender figure.

'I eat well. I can't help being naturally skinny,' she muttered.

Her mind was focused on the first part of the doctor's statement and she did a frantic calculation. Her period was only a couple of days late. There was no need to panic, she told herself. No need for the sick dread that had settled in the pit of her stomach when she remembered how she had woken the last two mornings feeling horribly sick. The possibility that she could be pregnant was too terrifying to contemplate. She could *not* have conceived by accident a second time, she assured herself. Lightning couldn't strike twice.

She was convinced that she must be suffering from a gastric virus.

'Where do you think you're going?' Drago demanded as he walked back into the room after the doctor had departed.

'To my room.' Jess shot a glance at him and felt her heart give a familiar flip as she recalled the conversation they'd had before she had fainted. She was no wiser as to what sort of relationship he wanted with her, but tonight she felt too weak and vulnerable to press him for an explanation. 'I think it will be better if I sleep alone. I'm sure I've picked up a stomach bug, and I don't want to disturb you if I'm ill during the night.'

He shook his head and, ignoring her protest, lifted her and deposited her back on the bed. 'I'm not risking you being alone in case you faint again. Hopefully the doctor will have some answers as to what is wrong with you tomorrow, but tonight you're sleeping in here, where I can keep an eye on you. *Madonna!*' Drago's patience evaporated as she slid off the mattress. 'You are the most stubborn, infuriating woman—'

'I need to take my dress off.'

Without another word he turned her round and ran the zip down her spine. It was ridiculous to feel shy when she had spent every night of the past weeks in his bed, Jess thought wryly. But she could not prevent a soft flush spreading across her cheeks as Drago slid the straps over her shoulders and tugged the dress down until it pooled at her feet.

Her breasts had felt ultra-sensitive recently, and her nipples were as hard as pebbles. Drago's eyes narrowed and Jess found herself holding her breath, willing him to take her in his arms and make the world go away. When he made love to her she could pretend that it was more than just good sex, and that maybe he really *did* want more than a casual affair with her. To her disappointment he moved away, and a moment later handed her one of his shirts.

'You'd better wear this to sleep in,' he said, without giving an explanation of why he wanted her to cover up when she usually slept naked. 'Would you like a drink? I'll ask Francesco to bring a pot of tea, if you like.'

For some inexplicable reason his gentle concern made Jess feel like bursting into tears, and only by biting down hard on her lip was she able to control her emotions.

'I don't want anything, thanks. I'm very tired.' *Drained* would be a better description, she thought as she climbed into bed. The silk sheets were deliciously cool, and she closed her eyes and gave a deep sigh that, unbeknown to her, increased Drago's concern.

Jess looked ethereally fragile, lying in the huge bed, with her fiery hair so bright in contrast to her pale face, he thought grimly. Until the doctor could come up with an explanation of what was wrong with her he was not going to let her set foot outside the *palazzo*—not to go back to London and her job as a decorator. He still had difficulty imagining her climbing ladders and painting walls for a living. Not because he thought that being a decorator was demeaning, but because her petite, slender figure was not suited to a physically demanding job.

As he joined her in the bed his body reacted predictably to the feel of her small, round bottom pressed up against him. He was thankful he had persuaded her to wear his shirt. She would tempt a saint, let alone a mortal man who was painfully aroused, he thought ruefully. The steady sound of her breathing told him that she had fallen asleep. Hopefully she would feel better after a restful night, so long as she did not have another of her disturbing dreams or weep silently in her sleep as she sometimes did. When he had asked her more about the dreams she had insisted she did not remember, but he sensed that she had not told him the whole truth, and he felt frustrated that she clearly did not trust him enough to confide in him.

Jess opened her eyes to find sunshine flooding the bedroom. Frowning, she glanced at the clock and was shocked to see that it was ten a.m. She had never slept so late in her life, but the long sleep must have done her good because she did not feel sick this morning. The panic she'd felt the previous night when she'd realised her period was a couple of days late seemed a silly overre-action. In fact she often felt nauseous and over-emotional just before her monthly period, and she wouldn't be surprised if it started today.

'How are you feeling?'

Drago's deep voice made her jump, and she turned her head to see him sitting in an arm-chair. Dressed in immaculately tailored beige chinos and a black polo shirt, his silky hair falling onto his brow and his square jaw bearing a faint shadow of dark stubble, he was so incredibly handsome that her heart performed its usual somersault. At first glance he appeared relaxed, with his long legs stretched out in front of him, his elbows resting on the arms of the chair and his fingers linked together. But closer inspection revealed the tense line of his jaw, and his black eyes were as hard as jet and curiously expressionless.

'I feel fine,' Jess assured him. 'I don't know why I fainted last night. Maybe I am a bit anaemic, as the doctor suggested.'

'*Santa Madre!*' He leapt to his feet with the violent force of a volcanic eruption. 'You can stop the pretence that you don't know what is wrong with you. I know you are pregnant with my child,' he said savagely. 'Why didn't you tell me?'

Scalding fury coursed through Drago's veins. Ever since he had received the phone call from the doctor an hour ago rage had been building inside him like steam in a pressure cooker, and now he exploded. Why had Jess kept her pregnancy a secret? Memories of the nightmare scenario that had happened eight years ago returned to haunt him. He would never forget Vittoria's terrified face—or the blood. There had been so much blood. He closed his eyes in an attempt to blot out the images, and when he opened them again he focused grimly on Jess.

'Tell me—were you planning to keep my child a secret from me for ever?' he demanded bitterly. He watched the colour drain from her face until she was even paler than she had been the previous night. 'Are you going to faint? Put your head between your knees.' His voice roughened with concern as he strode over to the bed and tangled his fingers in her bright hair, holding her head down so that the blood rushed back to her brain.

'I'm all right.' Jess drew a shuddering breath,

conscious of the painful thud of her heart as it jerked erratically against her ribcage. Her head was still spinning as she lifted her eyes to Drago. Intense shock made her skin feel clammy and strangled her vocal cords, so that her voice emerged as a shaky whisper. 'I'm not pregnant. I can't be.'

Drago frowned. Jess shocked reaction was clearly genuine, and his anger faded with the realisation that she had been unaware that she was expecting his baby.

'We both know we took a risk once and had unprotected sex the first night we slept together,' he said in a softer tone. 'Dr Marellis phoned earlier this morning, while you were still asleep, and confirmed that your blood test gave a positive result for pregnancy.'

Jess's mouth felt parched. 'He had no right to give you confidential information about me.'

'Eduardo is an old family friend. Presumably he believed I had a right to know that you are carrying my child, and he congratulated me on my impending fatherhood.'

Jess shook her head, as if she could somehow

dismiss his words. *It couldn't be true*, she thought frantically. But why would Drago lie? Maybe the doctor was wrong about the test result? She knew she was clutching at a very fragile straw. A blood test to detect pregnancy was almost one hundred per cent likely to be accurate.

'I swear I didn't know,' she said numbly. 'I'm only a few days late and I didn't think anything of it.'

That wasn't absolutely true, she admitted silently. The nausea she had been experiencing in recent days had seemed frighteningly familiar, but she had been too scared to think about a possible cause. It had been easier to ignore her suspicions. But now she could not hide from the devastating truth. She had conceived Drago's child—and from his furious expression he was no more pleased by the news than Seb had been when she had told him she was expecting *his* baby.

Jess began to tremble as reaction set in. She was going to have a baby. It was something she had assumed would never happen again. The trauma she had experienced as a teenager had left mental scars, and the memory of that terrible time, the desperate decision she had made, caused her to clench her fingers until her knuckles were white.

There was no doubt that she would go ahead with the pregnancy. Her acceptance of that fact was instant and resolute. But she had to face the bleak reality that her situation was no better than it had been years ago, when she was seventeen. She was older, and she had a job, she reminded herself. At least she had the means to support a child—although how she would manage to work as a decorator when she was heavily pregnant or with a newborn baby in tow was a problem she would have to face along with many others.

Caught up in her thoughts, she gave a start when Drago moved to stand by the window. His hard-boned profile looked so intimidating. She bit her lip. If only things had been different. If only they were lovers in the true sense of the word, and instead of standing stiffly on the other side of the room he had taken her in his arms and told her he was overjoyed that his child was developing inside her. Poor baby, she thought, and her heart splintered. She squeezed her eyes shut to prevent the sudden stinging tears from falling as she was overwhelmed by guilt. Two mistakes, two unplanned pregnancies, and two little lives affected by her stupidity.

'What are you thinking?' Drago turned back to face Jess, resenting the urgent, shaming desire that kicked in his gut as he studied her delicate beauty and the vibrant hair that fell past her shoulders in a rippling stream of red-gold silk. How could he be fantasising about making love to her when she looked so fragile that she might snap? he asked himself angrily. His only consideration should be for the child she was carrying inside her.

She gave a helpless shrug. 'I'm thinking about how I'll manage as a single mother. As long as I stay fit and healthy there's no reason why I shouldn't carry on working full-time until just before the baby is due. And afterwards—well, babies sleep a lot for the first few months, and I'm sure I'll be able to take the pram on site—'

She broke off as Drago growled something in

Italian. She guessed it was probably lucky she did not understand.

'If you think I would allow you to take my child onto a building site you are even crazier than I believed when I caught you climbing down from the balcony of your room,' he said harshly.

Her pale cheeks flushed with temper at his bossiness. 'I don't work on building sites. I decorate houses. I don't build them. I realise it won't be ideal to take the baby with me, but how else do you expect me to manage? I'll have to work to support the baby.'

'No, you will not. As my wife you will not want for anything. I will provide more than adequately for you and my child.'

Jess stiffened, sure that she could not have heard Drago correctly. 'What do you mean, as your wife?' she asked unsteadily.

'Naturally I will marry you,' he stated, in a coolly arrogant tone. His brows rose when she made a choked sound. 'It is the obvious solution.'

'Not to me, it isn't.' She bit her lip. 'Last night you said you wanted our relationship to continue, but you had no intention of marrying me, did you?' she said shrewdly.

'That was different. Last night I did not know that you are carrying my heir,' he replied bluntly.

'Your *heir*!' She quickly looked down at her fingers, which she had unknowingly been twisting together, determined not to let him see how much his comment hurt. Of course the only reason he was considering marrying her was for the sake of his child. 'I'm expecting your baby, Drago—a tiny new human being that in a few months' time will take his or her first breath of life. It's rather too early to be planning the baby's role as CEO of Cassa de Cassari.'

Jess's description of the new life developing inside her touched a chord deep inside Drago and brought home to him as nothing else had the astounding, amazing reality that in a few months from now she would give birth to his child. Her pregnancy was unplanned and totally unexpected. She had seemed so certain she could not have conceived the first time they had slept together. But now, with irrefutable proof that she had not been protected, he was trying to come to terms with how he felt.

Immediately after his telephone conversation with the doctor he had been stunned—and, if he was honest, dismayed. His life was already busy enough, without the additional responsibilities that having a child would bring. But, like it or not, Jess's pregnancy was a reality he needed to deal with. She was carrying the Cassari heir and he had a duty towards her and the child. His decision to marry her was not only driven by a sense of duty, Drago acknowledged. Now that his shock was fading he felt excited, somewhat overwhelmed, but ultimately delighted by the prospect that he was going to be a father.

The doctor had confirmed that the baby was due in January. As long as all went well with Jess's pregnancy, Drago reminded himself. His euphoria faded as memories of Vittoria's pregnancy returned to haunt him. He would always feel guilty that he had not paid her enough attention or taken proper care of her. He would not make the same mistake again, he vowed. Jess would receive the best medical care.

Her talk of working during her pregnancy sent a shaft of fear through him. She was so hot-headed and independent. He could not risk her deciding to go back to England to run her decorating company. The only practical solution, whereby he could keep a close eye on her during her pregnancy *and* be a full-time father to his child once it was born, was to persuade her to marry him.

'I'm not thinking of the baby's possible future role within the company. After what happened with Angelo I will not put the pressure of expectation on my child,' he said ruefully. 'But this baby will be a member of the Cassari family, and he or she has a right to grow up here at the *palazzo*. It is also our child's right to be loved and cared for by both its parents. Surely, after growing up in a children's home, you must agree that the best thing we can do for our child is to provide a stable family unit?'

Shaken by the fervour in his voice, Jess felt a lump form in her throat. All her life she had longed to be part of a family, and of course she wanted that security for her baby. But it had not crossed her mind that Drago would want his child, let alone that he would suggest they should marry. She knew he was not talking about the sort of marriage that featured in romantic films and fairy tales. He had not mentioned love. Was it foolish to want to be loved? she thought painfully. Was it selfish to wish that she mattered to someone?

'We can give the baby security without getting married,' she said quietly. 'We could lead separate lives but still share parenting responsibilities.'

'You mean we could go to court and argue over access rights and which of us the child will spend Christmases and birthdays with?' Drago's voice deepened. 'Is that the best we can offer the little person we have created, who shares your blood and mine, *cara*?'

Jess bit her lip. She wondered if Drago had deliberately played on her ragged emotions with his evocative words. He did not know that she had once made the hardest decision a mother could make so that her child would have the best possible life. Now she was being asked to make another difficult decision—this time to marry a man who did not love her for the sake of the child she carried.

The strident ring of his phone shattered the tense silence that had fallen between them. Muttering a curse, Drago glanced at the caller display and frowned. 'It's Dorotea. I'd better speak to her.'

After a brief conversation in Italian he ended the call and glanced at Jess. 'Angelo is to undergo more surgery on his leg this morning. My aunt wants me to go to the hospital, but I told her I have something important to deal with here.'

'I think you should go,' Jess said quickly. 'Your family need you. Dorotea must be so worried.'

'I'm not leaving you while we have issues to resolve,' Drago told her fiercely. 'You, and the child you are carrying, are the most important things right now. I have asked you to marry me and I need your answer, Jess.'

The huskiness in his voice tugged on Jess's emotions, and she swallowed the lump in her throat. Part of her wanted to accept Drago's proposal. He had sounded as though he meant it when he'd said she was important to him, but she reminded herself that it was the baby he cared about—not her. The idea of giving up her life in London, her independence, and agreeing to marry a man who did not love her was not a decision she could make lightly, and the fact that she was in love with Drago made that decision even harder.

She lifted her eyes to his handsome face and knew she needed to be alone while she considered her options. 'I want some time on my own to think,' she said quietly. 'Marriage is an enormous step, and I need to be sure in my mind that it is the right thing to do.'

Something in her voice made Drago control his frustration. It was true that marriage was a big step, he acknowledged. Yet strangely he did not find the prospect of giving up his playboy lifestyle and committing himself to a long-term relationship with Jess unwelcome. She was the mother of his child, and for that reason the decision to marry her was an easy one to make.

He wanted to stay with her and try to allay her doubts, but she had asked to be alone and he had to respect her request. 'You're right. I should go to the hospital and try to keep Aunt Dorotea calm,' he said abruptly. 'God knows, she has suffered enough stress lately.' He walked over to the bed and stared down at Jess. 'We'll continue this conversation later.' He leaned over her and captured her mouth in a brief, hard kiss. 'But I warn you, *cara*, I will do everything I possibly can to persuade you to be my wife.'

Hours later Jess could still feel the imprint of Drago's lips on hers. He would not have to try very hard to persuade her to marry him, she acknowledged ruefully. One kiss turned her to putty in his hands—which was why she was glad she had insisted on him giving her time to think about his proposal.

The *palazzo*'s gardens were an oasis of green tranquillity in the heart of Venice. Usually she loved to sit beside the ornamental pool and watch the goldfish dart beneath the water lilies, but as the afternoon slipped towards evening her thoughts were still confused and she found no sense of peace in her beautiful surroundings. She knew that for the baby's sake the sensible option would be to accept a marriage of convenience with her child's father, but her heart ached at the prospect of being Drago's unwanted wife. Would it be possible to sustain a relationship built solely on passion? Jess feared not. And when Drago's desire for her faded would he seek his pleasure elsewhere? Oh, she was sure he would be discreet, but the idea of him having affairs with other women was unbearable.

'Francesco tells me you have been out here for most of the day. I hope you kept out of the sun?'

Jess whipped her head round at the sound of Drago's voice, and her heart lurched as she watched him striding across the garden towards her. What chance did her heart stand when he was so impossibly gorgeous? she thought wryly. As he sat down on the bench beside her she tore her eyes from him and pretended to study the fish in the pool.

'How is Angelo?'

'The surgery went well, and now that the plaster cast has been removed from his leg the consultant is hopeful that he can be discharged from hospital in a week or so.'

'Good…that's great news. I'm sure he's pleased.' She didn't know what to say to him, and sticking to the topic of his cousin's recovery seemed a safe option.

'Jess…' Drago could not hide the faint impatience in his voice. 'Much as I care about my cousin, my only interest right now is whether you have reached a decision.' He slid his hand beneath her chin and tilted her face so that he could look into her troubled green eyes. 'I can see you still have doubts. Talk to me, *cara*, and tell me what is holding you back.'

'I don't belong in your world,' she muttered, voicing one of her biggest worries. 'Aren't you concerned that I won't be a suitable wife for you? I proved at the party last night that I am a hopeless hostess.' She flushed as she remembered her awkward attempts to talk to the guests and her clumsiness at the dinner table.

Drago frowned. 'That's not true. Many people remarked on how charming you were, and how much they enjoyed chatting with you.'

Jess wasn't convinced. 'You can't get away from the fact that I am the daughter of a drunk, not a member of the Italian aristocracy. Theresa Petronelli told me you were once engaged to a woman called Vittoria whose father is a count. I know she is very beautiful and sophisticated because she featured on the front cover of that magazine that you saw when we were in St Mark's Square.'

He shrugged, but beneath his casual air Jess sensed sudden tension. 'It's no secret that at one time Vittoria and I planned to marry. But it didn't happen. She ended our engagement and now she is happily married to another man. I'll be honest and admit that until I received the phone call from Dr Marellis this morning I had no great desire to marry,' he said bluntly. 'But knowing that you are expecting my baby has changed everything. I don't want my child to be born illegitimate. I know it is not considered important these days, but to me it matters a great deal that my child will bear my name.'

He grimaced when he saw the doubtful expression in Jess's eyes. 'I know you don't have happy memories of your father, but I swear to you that I will not be like him.' He took her cold hands in his strong, warm ones. 'I will love our child with all my heart,' he promised, 'and I will be the best father I can possibly be.' He would not fail at this second chance to be a father, Drago vowed silently. He would not fail this child.

Jess stared at their linked hands through eyes blurred with tears. Perhaps pregnancy was making her feel emotional. She hadn't cried since… She drew a swift breath as she was bombarded with memories that still had the power to make her weep.

Seven years ago, after Seb had made it clear that he wanted nothing to do with the child she had conceived by him, she hadn't known what to do. She had felt alone and scared. But now, with Drago, she did not have to fear the future. He had promised to take care of her and the baby, and as the full implications of his offer to marry her sank in she felt an overwhelming sense of relief. There was no need for her to worry about how she would manage to bring up a child on her own, and no need for her to make a terrible choice like the one she had made seven years ago.

'I suppose you will want me to sign a prenuptial agreement?' she muttered. 'It makes sense for you to protect your assets should we decide to…to divorce.'

She caught her bottom lip with her teeth as he slid his hand beneath her chin and gently forced her to meet his steady gaze.

'I'm not planning for us to divorce. I am prepared to make a lifelong commitment to you as well as to our child.' Drago stood up and drew her to her feet, his midnight-dark eyes focused intently on her face. 'What is your answer, Jess?'

All that mattered was the baby, she reminded herself fiercely. So she would have a husband who did not love her? Well, there were many worse things in life. Drago's avowal that he viewed marriage to her as a lifelong commitment gave her some measure of reassurance, but even so her heart was hammering hard against her ribs and she found it difficult to breathe as she said unsteadily, 'All right…I'll marry you.'

CHAPTER TEN

'AT THE END of this month! Why do you want us to get married so quickly?'

Her expression tense, Jess twisted the enormous diamond solitaire ring on her finger. For the past week she had tried to ignore the reservations she still had about accepting Drago's proposal, but when he had slid the engagement ring onto her finger a few moments ago she had been gripped by panic. She had always known he was powerful and commanding, but the speed with which he was organising everything and taking over her life was frightening. Her common sense told her she was doing the right thing for the baby, but Drago's determination to rush ahead with the wedding, and the way he bulldozed any objections she voiced, made her feel trapped.

He shrugged. 'What reason is there to wait?

You are expecting my baby and I want to make you my wife as soon as possible.'

'But what if…?' Jess's voice faltered. 'I'm very early in my pregnancy. What if something goes wrong and there *is* no baby? We will have married for no reason.'

Drago's expression was hidden beneath his heavy lids. 'Nothing will go wrong,' he stated with fierce conviction, as if he dared fate to argue with him. 'The doctor said after he examined you this morning that you are fit and healthy—although you need to put on a bit of weight. From now on I am going to make sure you eat properly,' he added in a warning tone. 'You also need to get plenty of rest—especially in the early months while the baby is developing. I don't want you to do too much, or feel stressed. That's why it is best for us to have the wedding soon. And you won't have to worry about the arrangements. I'll take care of everything.'

Drago was certainly taking his duties as a prospective father seriously, Jess thought with a sigh. It was rather nice to receive so much attention from him after a lifetime of fending for herself, but she knew his only concern was for the baby—which meant that while she was pregnant he was concerned for her well-being too. Of course she was glad that he was going to be a devoted father. After her own miserable experiences, growing up with her alcoholic father and then in the children's home, she was relieved that her baby would have a very different childhood from the one she'd had. But it would be nice if Drago cared for *her* a little, rather than regarding her as an incubator, she thought wistfully.

From the sound of it she was not going to have much say regarding what sort of wedding she would like. She could imagine his reaction if she told him she had always dreamed of getting married on a white sandy beach, barefoot, with flowers in her hair. The huge, blindingly brilliant diamond engagement ring was an indication that the wedding would have no expense spared, and she assumed that the guest list would be made up of his sophisticated friends.

'Are you ready to go down to dinner? You're not feeling sick again, are you?' Drago frowned when he saw how pale Jess was. 'I thought morning sickness was called that for a reason,' he said drily.

'It can happen at any time of the day. I used to—' She stopped abruptly.

'Used to what?' he demanded, puzzled by her sudden, palpable tension.

'I…I used to have a friend who was sick at all times of the day when she was pregnant.' Jess could feel herself blushing. She was not a natural liar, and she could tell from the speculative look Drago gave her that he was not convinced by her explanation. To her relief he did not pursue the matter.

'I can arrange for your dinner to be served up here, if you would prefer it?'

'No, I feel fine. Besides, I want to see Angelo on his first evening home from the hospital. He's going to be surprised when he hears about us.'

'My cousin is delighted—as are my mother and aunt.'

'You mean you've told them already?'

Ever since she had agreed to marry Drago, Jess had suffered badly from pregnancy sickness and had not left his wing of the *palazzo* or seen Luisa and Dorotea. She had assumed that he would wait until she was with him to announce their engagement, but clearly that had not been the case. He was like a steamroller, driving forcefully towards his goal—which in this case was marriage to the mother of his child, Jess thought dismally. Once again she felt a sense of panic that she was trapped and powerless against his formidable strength of will.

'Of course I informed my family of our intention to marry,' he said coolly. 'They are all delighted about the baby.' He hesitated, and to Jess's surprise streaks of colour flared along his sharp cheekbones. 'My family are under the impression that our marriage is a love-match.' The expression in his dark eyes was faintly challenging. 'I don't want them to be disappointed.'

Jess could not hide her confusion. 'I don't understand. Are you saying that they think we are...' she stumbled over the words '...in love? Why don't you tell them that we're marrying for the baby's sake?'

'It is precisely for the baby's sake that I haven't explained the nature of our relationship.' When

Jess frowned, Drago continued coolly. 'Babies do not stay babies for very long. They grow up fast. And children are very perceptive. Do you want our child to have the pressure of knowing that we married purely for their sake? If it is believed by everyone that we married for love then there will be no risk of our child feeling that we sacrificed our happiness for him or her.'

Jess bit her lip. Did Drago feel that by marrying her he was sacrificing his happiness? If so, how on earth were they going to give a convincing performance that they were in love? she wondered.

He drew back the cuff of his dinner jacket and glanced at the gold Rolex on his wrist. 'We should go down for dinner. Before we go, I want to say how beautiful you look, *mia bella*,' he murmured, his eyes darkening as he studied her. The emerald silk strapless dress revealed her slim white shoulders, she had piled her hair into a loose knot on top of her head and, unbeknown to Jess, she looked so exquisitely lovely that desire corkscrewed through Drago.

Still smarting from the idea that he viewed

marriage to her as a sacrifice, she stalked over to the door with her head held high, and said coolly, 'Presumably we don't have to start the pretence that we are in love until we are in front of your family? Although, to be honest, I'm not sure I'm that good an actress.'

'Perhaps this will help you get into character.' He caught up with her and spun her round, stifling her angry protest with his mouth as he lowered his head and claimed her lips in a searing kiss that left her trembling and breathless.

It was over far too quickly, and to compound Jess's shame Drago had to unfurl her fingers from the lapels of his jacket as he stepped away from her.

'Keep responding to me like that and you'll even convince *me* that I'm the love of your life, *cara*,' he mocked gently, and without giving her a chance to reply he put his hand in the small of her back and steered her out of the room.

Jess's face still felt hot when Drago ushered her into the dining room. Running her tongue over her lips, she felt their slight puffiness and knew she must look as though she had been thoroughly kissed by her fiancé.

Seeing Angelo, balanced on crutches and looking drawn but otherwise remarkably well, provided a welcome distraction—although his greeting, 'Here are the two lovebirds,' brought another flush to her cheeks.

Aunt Dorotea rushed up and enveloped her in a hug. Angelo's mother was convinced that Jess had been responsible for her son regaining his memory and she congratulated the newly engaged couple effusively. Drago's mother was more reserved with her congratulations, and not for the first time Jess was conscious of Luisa studying her speculatively.

After dinner she cornered Jess in the conservatory. 'I'm surprised by your choice of engagement ring,' she murmured, lifting Jess's hand and studying the enormous diamond. 'This bauble seems a little too ostentatious for your tastes.'

'I didn't choose it,' Jess admitted. 'Drago...surprised me when he gave it to me. And I think it's absolutely lovely,' she lied.

For some strange reason she found that she did

not want to be disloyal to Drago. Luisa had been right to guess that the ring wasn't her taste, but she certainly didn't want to risk hurting Drago's feelings by saying so.

Luisa looked at her closely. 'So you really do love him?' she murmured. For the first time that evening she smiled warmly at Jess, who had gone bright red. 'I am very happy for both of you.' Her voice became serious. 'May I offer you a word of advice? I adore my son, but Drago is strong-willed—like his father—and you may find it necessary to stand up to him from time to time.' She smiled again. 'But don't let him know I told you that.'

Jess was still reeling because Luisa had guessed how she felt about Drago. 'I won't,' she promised. 'I'm strong-willed myself, and we've already had a few clashes,' she said ruefully.

'It won't do him any harm. Vittoria was too soft-natured for him, and had they married they would not have been happy. But I was sorry their relationship ended so tragically. It took Drago a long time to get over what happened. I expect he has told you—' Luisa broke off as Drago entered the conservatory.

'I've been looking for you,' he said as he walked over to them and slid his arm around Jess's waist. 'I missed you, *tesoro*.'

His velvet-soft voice, and the gentle look in his eyes as he stared down at her caused Jess's heart to lurch. His performance as an adoring fiancé was very convincing, and she had to remind herself sternly that it was an act for his family's benefit. But she wished he had not interrupted her conversation with his mother, for she was none the wiser about why his engagement to Vittoria had ended.

Did he still love the beautiful socialite? she wondered later as she followed him into the bedroom. He had sounded regretful when he had explained that Vittoria had been the one to break off their engagement. What had Drago's mother meant when she'd said his engagement to Vittoria had ended 'tragically'?

Frustrated that there was so much she did not know about the man she was to marry in two weeks' time, Jess watched him shrug off his dinner jacket and begin to unfasten his shirt buttons, revealing inch by inch the muscular bronzed chest covered with whorls of dark hair that arrowed over his flat abdomen and disappeared beneath the waistband of his trousers. His devastating good looks took her breath away, and a different kind of frustration unfurled in the pit of her stomach.

He glanced over at her, and Jess glimpsed a predatory hunger in his eyes which was quickly masked beneath the sweep of his thick lashes. But the glittering look lifted her spirits, because it was proof that Drago's desire for her had not faded. They had been drawn together by their fierce sexual attraction to each other, and it was likely that desire was all he would ever feel for her, she acknowledged sadly. But it was better than nothing, and life had taught Jess to settle for what she could get and not wish for the moon.

'Did I mention how gorgeous you look in that dress?' Drago murmured.

'You told me before we went down to dinner,' she reminded him.

Rosy pink colour flared on her cheeks, and

Drago knew she was remembering him kissing her. She had goaded him so that he had lost his self-control and punished her with a searing kiss, but his anger had quickly turned to desire and he had spent the evening in a state of uncomfortable semi-arousal.

She was a work of art—so slender and fine-boned that she reminded him of a delicate porcelain figurine. But her bare shoulders were satin-soft beneath his fingers as he traced the line of her collarbone, and the pulse jerking at the base of her throat was evidence that she was a warm, responsive woman, not a cold statue. Her eyes glowed emerald-bright and her mouth was a soft pink temptation that he could not resist. He felt his body stir, and his need for her pounded an urgent drumbeat through his veins.

He cupped her face in his hands, but a frown drew his brows together when he noticed the purple shadows beneath her eyes. She looked infinitely fragile. His frown deepened. What was he thinking of, putting his own selfish need for sexual fulfilment before her well-being? And not only *her* well-being, but that of the child in her belly. How could he consider making love to her during these crucial early days of her pregnancy? Drago asked himself angrily. He knew better than most how precarious was the tiny life she carried.

Ignoring the ache of frustration in his gut, he dropped his hands from her shoulders. 'You should get to bed. You look all in,' he murmured. 'Here.' He took one of his shirts from a drawer and handed it to her. The look of disappointment in her eyes tested his resolve, and Drago knew there was no way he would be able to keep his hands off her if he had to lie next to her delectable body all night. 'I need to read a report that won't keep. I don't want to disturb you, so I'll sleep in my dressing room tonight.'

'There's no need for you to do that,' Jess mumbled, taken aback by his sudden change from sensual lover to enigmatic stranger. So much for her belief that there would at least be passion in their marriage, if not love, she thought bleakly. Drago was in such a hurry to get away from her that he was already walking through the door leading to his dressing room.

He turned back to her, his expression serious. 'It is important for the baby's development that you sleep well. But every night you have dreams that upset you, and you speak of someone called Katie.' He waited for Jess to make a response, and when she remained silent frustration surged through him. He sensed there was something in her past that she was keeping secret, but he could not force her to confide in him, he acknowledged heavily. 'I'll check with Dr Marellis if it is harmful to experience disturbing dreams during pregnancy,' he said gruffly. '*Buonanotte*, Jess.'

I'll check with Dr Marellis was a phrase Drago repeated often during the following days, and his obsessive concern for her health drove Jess mad. He consulted an array of health care books, monitored every aspect of her pregnancy, and fretted about her bouts of morning sickness, which grew worse daily and left her feeling weak and drained.

'How can you be sure it is normal to be so sick?' he demanded when she tried to reassure him. She almost let slip that this was not her first experience of morning sickness. But the idea of talking about her first pregnancy was too painful to contemplate when the wound in her heart was so deep and raw.

Even when Drago was abroad she still felt stifled by him, Jess brooded, three days before their wedding was due to take place. He had explained that his business trip to Germany was unavoidable. She had refrained from admitting that she would be glad to have a few days to herself. But her hopes of having some time alone, so that she could come to terms with the dramatic changes in her life and especially her feelings about her pregnancy, had been dashed by Drago's constant phone calls.

'Yes, I ate breakfast,' she told him patiently. 'No, I haven't been sick this morning.'

'Why not?' His voice sounded sharp over the phone. 'Why would the sickness suddenly stop?'

'I don't know. I'm just glad to have kept my food down for once,' Jess muttered. Really, there was no pleasing him, she thought irritably. According to Drago, she was either too sick or not sick enough.

'Yes—that's good, of course. Perhaps you'll start to put on weight rather than lose it. But I'll call Eduardo Marellis and arrange for him to come to the *palazzo* and check that your pregnancy is progressing as it should.'

'There's no need. I only saw him four days ago.'

'It's better to be safe,' Drago said in the uncompromising voice Jess knew so well. 'I don't want you to do too much today. In fact why don't you spend the morning in bed?'

It was on the tip of Jess's tongue to tell him that being in bed on her own wasn't much fun, but pride kept her quiet. Drago had slept in his dressing room every night since he had announced their engagement to his family, and she was determined to hide how hurt she felt and how much she missed him. It wasn't just the sex; it was the feeling of closeness to him that she longed for— because then she could fool herself that he cared for her a little.

When he ended the phone call she wandered over to the window and stared out at the view of the Grand Canal, which was busy with the boats and water taxis that provided the main mode of transport through the city. Venice attracted thousands of tourists in the summer, but Jess had lived her whole life in London and was used to busy streets. She was also used to being independent and going out when and where she pleased, but Drago had insisted that she did not leave the *palazzo* without being accompanied by his bodyguard Fico.

She felt as if she was imprisoned in a gilded cage, she thought heavily. She missed her freedom, and with her wedding only days away she felt trapped. Marrying Drago was undoubtedly the best thing she could do for the baby. Their child would enjoy a privileged lifestyle that she could not possibly give if she was a single mother. But she was struggling to come to terms emotionally with being pregnant for a second time, and the guilt she had buried for so long was a permanent ache in her heart.

If only she could just have a few hours to herself to think—without Fico or the other household staff hovering around her. She grimaced as she remembered her crazy attempt to climb down from the balcony the first night Drago had brought her to the *palazzo*. She was not going to do anything as stupid as that again, but there was no reason why she shouldn't slip away by herself for a couple of hours. Drago need never find out.

'What do you mean, she's not here?' Drago roared, venting his fury on the hapless maid who had hurried downstairs to tell him that Signorina Harper was not anywhere in the *palazzo* or the garden.

Dropping his briefcase on the marble floor of the entrance hall, he thrust his fingers through his hair and discovered that his hand was shaking. Fear was rapidly replacing the anger that had blazed in him when he had received a phone call from Fico to tell him that Jess had apparently disappeared.

Thank God he had decided to cut his trip to Germany short and had already been at Marco Polo airport when he had spoken to Fico. Drago glared at the bodyguard, who had just returned from St Mark's Square, which was one of Jess's favourite haunts.

'No sign of her,' Fico said gruffly. 'But the

place is packed with tourists and I could have missed her if she's in a café. I've left three members of the security team to continue searching—'

Puzzled by the bodyguard's abrupt silence, Drago followed his gaze and spun round to see Jess walking up the front steps of the *palazzo*. Relief caused his knees to sag, but incensed by the effect she had on him, and the unpalatable fact that she weakened and unmanned him, he strode forward to meet her.

'Where the *hell* have you been?' he demanded, his voice taut with fury. 'Why did you go out without Fico when I expressly forbade you to? Why did you disobey me?'

Several hours of walking about in the hot sunshine had left Jess feeling exhausted, but as she was subjected to Drago's verbal attack she forgot her tiredness and her temper simmered.

'You *forbade* me! I *disobeyed* you! Listen to yourself, Drago. They are not the words of a husband to his wife—at least not in any marriage I want to be part of. Why shouldn't I go out on my own? I only went to Murano to visit the glassblowers' workshops. What harm is there in that?'

She suddenly became aware that they were not alone. Several of the staff had been drawn to the hall by the sound of raised voices, and Fico was shifting from foot to foot, looking as though he would rather be anywhere but witnessing her argument with Drago.

'I am *not* going to stand here and allow you to *harangue* me in front of the staff,' she muttered, and she raced towards the staircase.

'Come back here.' Drago was beside her in an instant, and kept pace with her as she marched up the stairs.

When they reached the landing he scooped her into his arms and, ignoring her furious protest, strode into the suite of rooms they had shared since she had arrived at the *palazzo*.

'I'll tell you what harm there is in you jaunting off alone,' he growled, as he carried her through to the bedroom and dropped her onto the bed so hard that she bounced on the mattress. Before she could even think of trying to get up he leaned over her, imprisoning her against the satin bed cover. 'I am one of the wealthiest men in Italy. I attract a lot of media attention. And now that you are my fiancée, so do you,' he told her bitingly. 'Ever since a photo of us leaving Trattoria Marisa was published on the front page of several newspapers you have been at risk of being kidnapped by criminal gangs who would demand a huge ransom for your release. *That* is why Fico sticks to your side like glue.'

Jess swallowed, shaken not just by his words but by the intensity in his black eyes that told her the threat of kidnap was a very real and frightening possibility. 'I didn't think,' she whispered.

'It seems to be a persistent theme with you,' he said sardonically. He jerked away from her as if he could not bear to be near her. 'And I see you're not wearing your engagement ring again.'

Anger burned like acid in Drago's gut as he stared at her, sprawled on the bed, with her glorious hair spread across the satin bedspread. Wearing a simple white sundress that had rucked up to reveal her slim thighs, she was a beguiling mixture of innocence and earthy sensuality, and the idea that she would have attracted much male interest while she wandered around Venice filled him with rage.

'Did you go out without your ring so that you could flirt with other men?' he demanded savagely. 'Do I need to remind you that you are carrying *my* child?'

Stunned to see streaks of colour run along Drago's cheekbones, Jess shook her head. That could *not* be jealousy she had heard in his voice, she told herself. 'Of course I didn't go out to meet other men. And being sick constantly is enough of a reminder that I'm pregnant,' she said drily. 'I'm not used to wearing jewellery, and I find my ring a bit cumbersome for everyday wear, so I thought I would just put it on for social events.'

Realising the effort Jess was making to be tactful about the engagement ring that he had already guessed she did not like, Drago felt his anger fade. Most women he knew would love to own a diamond the size of a rock, but Jess was different from any other woman he'd ever met, he acknowledged wryly.

'Have you any idea how worried I was when Fico told me you had disappeared?' he asked raggedly. '*Dio*, I was scared. you had had an accident, or been taken ill.' He closed his eyes as memories of rushing to the hospital with Vittoria flooded his mind. 'Why did you go off like that?'

Jess bit her lip, overcome with guilt that her irresponsible behaviour had caused Drago to look so haggard. She knew how concerned he was for the baby.

'I needed some space. I'm used to being independent,' she mumbled. 'It has struck me in the last couple of days that Italy is going to be my home once we are married. I love Venice, but I miss London,' she admitted. 'You probably find it hard to understand, but I *like* running T&J Decorators, and I miss Mike and Gaz and the other guys I used to work with. I don't have a life of my own or friends in Venice. I especially miss my workshop and being able to do my woodcarving. You're smothering me,' she said in low tone. 'I understand that your interest—obsession, even—with my pregnancy is because you are concerned for the baby. But I'm not an invalid. Pregnancy is a perfectly natural state.'

'Unless something goes wrong,' Drago said harshly. 'I have witnessed how devastating the consequences can be if there is a problem during pregnancy. If I have been obsessive, it is because I want to do everything possible to take care of you and the baby.'

His jaw clenched and his voice roughened with emotion as he stated flatly, 'It is something that I bitterly regret I did not do for my first child.'

CHAPTER ELEVEN

SHOCK RAN THROUGH Jess as she absorbed Drago's statement. 'What do you mean?' she said unsteadily. 'What child?'

He exhaled slowly. 'While I was engaged to Vittoria she fell pregnant, but she did not tell anyone—including me.' Noticing Jess's confused expression, he said heavily, 'I'd better start from the beginning. I first met Vittoria when we were children. Our families were friends, and as we grew up we often used to meet at social events. My ill-fated love affair with Natalia, the exotic Russian woman who conned me and Cassa di Cassari out of a fortune, was humiliating, and I vowed that in future I would use my head and not my heart in relationships,' he explained grimly. 'I felt it was my duty to marry and produce an heir. Vittoria was beautiful and charming, and her family connections to Italian nobility made me decide that she would be the perfect wife.'

'It sounds a coldly clinical way to choose a wife,' Jess said, taken aback by his lack of emotion. 'Didn't you love her?'

'I cared for her and respected her.' Drago hesitated. 'But I did not love her as I should have done. A few years before I had been crazily in love with Natalia,' he admitted roughly. 'I met her while I was still grieving for my father, and I completely lost my heart to her.'

Jess nodded. 'I can understand that. I fell desperately in love with Seb when I was very vulnerable after my friend Daniel died.'

'Discovering how Natalia had betrayed me hurt like hell,' Drago continued. 'I never wanted to feel pain like that again. So it seemed eminently sensible to marry a woman I liked who shared my goals. Vittoria seemed to accept that I needed to devote time to running Cassa di Cassari.' He grimaced. 'It shames me to say that I did not devote the same amount of time to my relationship with her. I was unaware that she suffered badly from nerves and illogical fears and had, among other things, a phobia of hospitals.'

Drago strode restlessly around the room, his mind bombarded by memories that still haunted him. 'I had no idea that Vittoria had conceived my child. She showed no signs, and she said nothing until she started to bleed heavily. Only then did she admit that she was four months pregnant. Poor Vittoria was petrified,' he said raggedly. 'Initially it was thought that she was suffering a miscarriage, but she haemorrhaged severely and was rushed to hospital—where she was found to have a condition called placenta preavia. It is a complication during pregnancy, but in extreme cases it can lead to the death of the mother and the baby. Because Vittoria had not been for any prenatal checks her condition went undetected until she started to bleed. She almost lost her life.' His throat moved as he swallowed hard. 'And tragically she lost the baby.'

'I'm sorry,' Jess whispered, her heart aching for him and his ex-fiancée. 'To lose a child during pregnancy must be agonising.'

'I blamed myself.'

She shook her head. 'You could not have prevented what happened to Vittoria. You said yourself she suffered a rare complication with her pregnancy.'

'If I had paid her more attention she might have told me sooner that she was pregnant and I would have persuaded her to see a doctor,' Drago said, his voice raw with guilt. 'If I had taken better care of her then her condition would have been detected and her pregnancy would have been closely monitored. I did not realise how much I wanted a child until my baby died,' he confessed huskily. 'Vittoria was heartbroken, and I certainly did not blame her when she decided that she no longer wished to marry me. I felt I had failed her *and* our unborn child.'

He looked at Jess, his eyes blazing with emotion. 'That is why I am determined to do everything I can to ensure that the child you are carrying is born safely. I want this baby very much, but I don't know how you feel, Jess.' He frowned. 'You seem...distant. I get the feeling that you are unhappy about being pregnant and that maybe you do not want our baby.'

It was his words "our baby" that wrecked Jess. Unlike during her first pregnancy, she was not alone this time. This baby had a father who clearly would be devoted to his child. The knowledge made her glad, but also desperately sad that she had been unable to be a mother to her first child.

'Of course I want our baby,' she told Drago thickly. Tears blinded her and she felt a pain inside as though her heart had cracked. *'You have no idea how much I want to be a mother.'*

The storm had been building for a long time, and now it broke. She buried her face in her hands and her shoulders shook as sobs tore through her slender frame.

'Jess?' Shaken to the core to see her sobbing so uncontrollably, Drago strode over to the bed and lifted her into his arms. *'Cara*, don't cry. I'm sorry I upset you. I just wasn't sure how you felt about being pregnant.'

Once again he had misjudged her, he thought grimly. There was so much about this woman he was about to marry that he did not understand—so many secrets that she kept from him.

He could only hope that one day she would learn to trust him. For now all he could do was cradle her in his lap and wrap his arms tightly around her while she wept.

It was a long time before Jess regained a fragile hold on her emotions. She had never allowed herself to cry like that before, and now she felt drained. Glancing at Drago from beneath her lashes, she felt her heart clench when she saw the bleak expression in his eyes. She wondered if he was thinking about the baby he and his fiancée had lost. He was clearly still haunted by the tragedy, and he must have found it hard to talk about the circumstances that had led to the ending of his engagement to Vittoria.

Jess was touched that he obviously trusted her enough to confide in her about his painful memories. Trust was an important element in a relationship. She knew Drago was curious about the dreams that troubled her and caused her to cry out in her sleep. He had asked her several times who Katie was, and lately she had been tempted to tell him. But something held her back. Her troubled childhood and teenage years had left her wary of revealing her feelings, and deep down she was afraid that Drago would judge her badly for what she had done. She could not bear to see disgust or condemnation in his eyes. No one could understand the utter devastation she had felt when she had given her child away, and it was just too agonising for her to talk about.

She closed her eyes, as if she could banish the heartbreaking memories of her past, and slowly became aware of how comforting it felt to be held close to Drago's chest, listening to the steady beat of his heart beneath her ear. She could feel the warmth of his body through his silk shirt, and the scent of his aftershave teased her senses.

He was stroking her hair, threading his fingers through its length in a rhythmic motion that was soothing but also sensual. A tremor ran through her as he cupped her chin and tilted her face to his dark gaze. Jess's heart missed a beat when he gently brushed away the tears from her cheeks. Something was unfurling inside her, and she knew from the sultry gleam in his eyes that he felt it too. Desire beat a slow but insistent drum in her veins.

'Cara?' His breath whispered across her lips before he covered them with his own and kissed her long and sweet and with increasing passion until she trembled. 'Do you want this?' he asked in a voice roughened with need as he trailed his mouth down her throat.

'Yes,' she said honestly. 'But do you?' She gave him a troubled look. 'You haven't touched me since you found out I'm pregnant. I thought…I assumed you no longer found me attractive.'

Drago lay back on the bed, still holding her in his arms, and rolled over so that she was beneath him. 'Does this feel like I'm not turned on by you?' he said wryly as the solid ridge of his arousal straining beneath his trousers pushed against her pelvis. 'I have not dared sleep in the same bed as you because I knew I wouldn't be able to resist making love to you.' He frowned. 'I read that sex in the early days of pregnancy carries a small risk of causing a miscarriage.'

'Well, Dr Marellis told me that it was perfectly safe to make love while I'm pregnant,' Jess murmured. She caught her breath when Drago slid his hand beneath her tee shirt and skimmed it over her ribcage to curl his fingers possessively around one breast.

'In that case, do you think it's okay for me to do this…?' he said softly, smiling at her reaction when he stroked his thumb-pad across her nipple and it immediately hardened.

'Perfectly okay,' she gasped as he whipped her tee shirt over her head and closed his mouth around the taut peaks he had exposed. Pregnancy had made her breasts incredibly sensitive, and starbursts of pleasure shot through her as he flicked his tongue across one nipple and then its twin. After weeks of being denied him she was instantly aroused, and she gave a tiny embarrassed laugh when he tugged off her skirt and panties and dipped his finger into her honeyed sweetness.

Eagerly she helped him strip, and when he stretched his bronzed, naked body next to her she clung to him and tried to pull him on top of her.

'Not yet, *tesoro*,' he said softly and, moving down the bed, he eased her legs apart and lowered his head so that his mouth found the sensitive heart of her femininity.

Jess whimpered with delight at his skilled fore-play and the dedication with which he used his tongue to bring her to the edge of heaven. After her emotional breakdown she needed him to restore her, and she trembled with desire when the fierce glitter in his eyes told her the moment had come. But instead of entering her he rolled onto his back, taking her with him, and lifted her above him.

'This way you're in control,' he murmured, and groaned as she slowly took his swollen length inside her. 'I always knew that with those amazing green eyes you had to be a sorceress,' he said thickly.

And then there were no more words—just the sound of their quickening breaths and moans of pleasure as together they set a driving rhythm that quickly took them higher and higher, until with a sharp cry Jess shuddered with the sweet ecstasy of her climax. Seconds later Drago lost his battle to hold back the tidal wave of his need for this one unique woman, and he buried his face in Jess's fragrant hair as his big body shook with the force of his release.

She was the mother of his child, and soon she would be his wife. Those two things brought Drago a level of contentment he had not expected, and he felt a curious tug on his heart as he placed his hand possessively on Jess's flat stomach. Her pregnancy was unplanned but he had no regrets. He wanted his baby, and he wanted to marry his flame-haired firebrand.

He tensed as the realisation hit him. But after a moment he relaxed, and his mouth curved into a smile when he saw that Jess had fallen asleep with her head resting on his shoulder. She was so beautiful she made his insides ache. But as he watched a tear seeped from beneath her lashes and slid down her cheek, and she whispered a name. *Katie.*

They married in a small, pretty church tucked away down a narrow side street that few tourists had discovered. Jess was surprised, for she had expected the wedding to take place in a register office, and she was even more surprised when Drago's mother met her at the door of the church and handed her an exquisite bouquet of cream roses.

'I had no idea that my son is such an incurable romantic,' Luisa said drily. 'He said to tell you that he chose these to complement your dress.'

Jess swallowed the lump that had formed in her throat. 'They're perfect.' Her ivory silk wedding dress was a fairy-tale creation that had been made for her by the designer Torre Umberto. The fluid lines of the gown suited her slender figure, and the crystal-covered bodice sparkled in the sunshine of a Venetian summer's day.

But the biggest surprise came when she walked into the church with Fico, who was to give her away, and saw Mike, Gaz and the rest of her workforce from T&J Decorators gathered in the pews.

'Drago arrange for your friends to come,' Fico told her in a gruff whisper. 'He say it make you happy.'

As she reached the altar and lifted her eyes to Drago's handsome face Jess knew she was happier than she had ever been in her life—and the thought terrified her. In all the bleak years of her childhood she had not imagined happiness like this, and she felt she did not deserve it.

Drago did not love her, she reminded herself. He was only marrying her because she was expecting his baby. But the gentle expression in his eyes as he took her hand and the marriage service began filled her with hope that they could make their marriage work.

Remember how Seb betrayed you, she told herself sternly. She had fooled herself into believing that he cared for her, and the legacy of that mistake would haunt her for ever. But she could not prevent the frantic leap of her heart when Drago slid a gold wedding band onto her finger and followed it with an exquisite emerald and diamond ring in the shape of a flower.

'The solitaire ring was too big and showy for you,' he murmured. 'This suits your small hand much better, and the emeralds match the colour of your eyes.'

Emerging from the church as man and wife, they boarded a gondola decorated with roses, and as Drago kissed her and the wedding guests cheered Jess decided that fairy tales could come true after all.

The reception at the Palazzo d'Inverno was an informal affair, and she was able to spend time chatting with the guys from T&J Decorators. Mike, who had acted as foreman in her absence, had now taken over running the business.

'I'm glad things have worked out for you, Jess,' he told her. 'But me and the lads miss you. If you ever get bored of swanning around in a palace I'll always find you some work. You're one of the best chippies in the trade.'

'Thanks, but being a mother is the only job I'm going to want for a long time,' Jess replied, her eyes softening as she imagined holding her baby in her arms.

'I enjoyed meeting your friends,' Drago said later, as they drove across the bridge linking Venice to the mainland. They were on their way to his house in the Italian Alps, where they were to spend their honeymoon. 'Remind me of the name of the guy covered in tattoos?'

'You mean Stan the Van? He does most of the driving to job sites.'

'And the guy with spiky pink hair and a missing front tooth?'

Jess grinned. 'He's called Sharky because he's Australian and has a scar that he says is from where he was bitten by a shark, but no one believes him.' She hesitated. 'I know they're a bit rough round the edges, but they're great guys and they have been like a family to me.'

Drago glanced at her and felt again that curious tug on his insides as he thought how beautiful she looked in her wedding dress. 'Now you are a member of the Cassari family,' he said gently. 'But we'll go to London often, so that you can visit your friends. I own a penthouse in Park Lane.'

The address of his London apartment was a reminder that they came from different worlds, Jess thought ruefully. She couldn't help feeling worried again that she would not fit into his sophisticated lifestyle with his glamorous friends.

'By the way, Sebastian Loxley is in prison.'

She shot him a startled look. 'How do you know?'

'I hired someone to track him down.' Drago gave a grim smile. 'I wanted to have a…let's call it a *discussion*,' he said in a dangerous voice, 'about the way he treated you. But for now he's out of my reach—serving eight years for credit card fraud.'

'I'm glad,' Jess said shakily. 'At least while he's in prison he can't hurt anyone else.'

Tired after the hectic day, she slept for much of the three-hour drive to the north of Italy, and woke to find the car was winding up a steep road surrounded by mountains.

'Welcome to Casa Rosa,' Drago said as he pulled up on the driveway of a picturesque alpine lodge.

The lower slopes of the mountains were grassy meadows, but the highest peaks of the Alps were still covered in snow that reflected the fiery brilliance of the setting sun.

'I've never been this close to mountains before,' Jess murmured in an awed voice as she looked around at the breathtaking scenery.

'In the winter even the lower slopes are covered in snow.' Drago smiled at her. 'After the baby is born I'll teach you to ski, if you like.'

Jess gave him a puzzled look. 'But who would look after the baby while we were skiing?'

'We will employ a nanny. You'll need help with the baby. Although I intend to cut down my work commitments, I'll still need to spend time running the company.'

While he was speaking Drago led the way into the house—a charming lodge with low ceilings, wood-panelled walls and stripped-pine floorboards scattered with colourful rugs.

But Jess did not notice the quaint charm of the house as she said fiercely, 'I don't want a nanny. I'm perfectly capable of taking care of my baby.'

Seeing the light of battle in her eyes, Drago held back from telling her that he planned to hire a nanny so that he and Jess could enjoy some time together. Much as he was looking forward to being a father, he intended to be a very attentive husband. 'We'll discuss it another time,' he murmured. 'For now, I think you should go to bed. You must be tired after a busy day.'

'I slept in the car,' Jess reminded him, 'and I'm not at all tired.' Her heart missed a beat when he cupped her chin in his hand and tilted her face to his.

'Good. I'm not tired either.' His deep voice seemed to wrap around her like a cloak of crushed velvet. 'So, what do you think that two people who are on their honeymoon and who are not tired should do, *cara*?'

His mouth was tantalisingly close to hers. Jess licked her suddenly dry lips and watched his eyes blaze with feral hunger. 'I think they should go to bed,' she answered huskily.

'How can our marriage be anything but a success when we are clearly on the same wavelength?'

His sexy smile stole her breath. And then he kissed her and the world went away.

The master bedroom had a wall of glass that gave stunning views of the mountains. In the purple softness of dusk Drago removed her wedding dress and the tiny wisps of lacy underwear, and Jess helped him out of his grey wedding suit, her fingers clumsy with impatience as she undid his shirt buttons.

'My wife,' he said softly, testing the words.

They sounded good. Better than good. They sounded like the most beautiful words Drago had ever heard. But he wasn't ready to share his deepest thoughts with her when they were so new to him, and so he told her instead how beautiful she was as he kissed her mouth and her breasts, and the sweetly sensitive place between her thighs. And when she cried his name he lifted himself above her and sank his powerful erection into her slick heat so that they became one.

He made love to her with passion and an underlying tenderness that touched Jess's soul. And in the aftermath of their mutual pleasure, when he gathered her close to his chest and they watched the stars pinprick the night sky, she knew that he had captured her heart and would hold it prisoner for all time.

CHAPTER TWELVE

'Do you really use the hot tub in winter?' Jess asked the next day, as she and Drago relaxed in the frothing water of the tub, which was positioned on the terrace and afforded a stunning view of the surrounding mountains. 'It must be freezing, running back to the house through the snow in a towel.'

His eyes glinted wickedly. 'There are ways to quickly restore body heat,' he assured her. 'I'll give you a demonstration later.' He climbed out of the hot tub and pulled on a bathrobe. 'But first I have a surprise for you.'

'I feel bad that I haven't given you a wedding present,' Jess murmured as she wrapped a towel around her and followed him back to the house.

'In a few months you will give me a child, and that's the only gift I want.'

His words were a timely reminder that she was

only here at this beautiful mountain retreat as his wife because she had conceived his baby. Jess pushed the thought away when she saw a large wooden chest on the floor of the sitting room.

'My wood-carvings!' she said in delight.

'I had all your tools and the carvings that you kept in your workshop sent over from London,' Drago explained. 'I'm having a room prepared at the *palazzo* for you to use as a studio.'

Jess had opened the storage trunk and was on her knees searching through it.

Drago took out an exquisite carving of an eagle and inspected it with a growing sense of incredulity. 'Your work is amazing. The detail on this eagle's wings is astounding.' As he studied a carving of a lion, which was perfect in every detail, he recognised that Jess had a very special talent. 'Each piece must take hours to complete. Have you had any formal training in art?'

'No. I would have loved to study art at college,' she revealed wistfully, 'but when I left school I needed to work to support myself.'

Drago picked up another sculpture of a young child. The detail on the face was so perfect that the small wooden figure was uncannily lifelike. He was puzzled as he watched Jess take other figurines from the chest. There were seven in all, clearly of the same little girl at different stages of her life—from a tiny baby lying in a carved crib to a child standing on skis, smiling joyfully.

'These figurines are so beautiful, *cara*. Who is the child?' Drago stared intently at the wooden figure he was holding and then at Jess. 'She looks a little like you.'

'Do you think so?'

A tremor shook her voice, and the expression in her eyes was so bleak and full of pain that Drago drew a sharp breath.

'Jess, what's wrong? Why are you crying?'

He stretched out a hand to her, but she turned away and began to place the carvings back in the box. 'I'm not crying, and nothing is wrong.' She stood up and gave him a fiercely bright smile. 'Everything is wonderful,' Jess insisted.

But Drago sensed she was keeping something from him, and once again frustration surged through him that she did not feel able to reveal the secrets that he could tell haunted her.

'The weather is too nice for us to stay indoors. Let's go for a walk higher in the mountains.'

Beneath the request Drago caught an almost desperate plea in her voice. He was tempted to shake her, to *force* her to open up to him and explain the cause of the tears that she sought to hide from him. It was not surprising that Jess had trust issues after the diabolical way she had been treated by the lowlife scum who had seduced her when she had been a vulnerable teenager, he reminded himself, but surely she knew he was nothing like Sebastian Loxley?

Her lack of trust in him was tearing him apart, and with a savage oath he caught hold of her shoulder and spun her round to face him. 'Who is Katie?' he demanded urgently.

His instincts told him that the name Jess cried out in her sleep, a person she denied she knew, was the cause of the raw anguish in her eyes. He glanced at the wooden figurine he was still holding and somehow knew it had a connection to Katie. The little wooden child had been carved with such infinite care, such *love*.

He stared at Jess, and his gut clenched when

he saw her fearful expression. *'Tesoro,'* he said thickly, 'do you really think I could ever hurt you?'

She swallowed and shook her head. 'No,' she whispered.

Drago released his breath slowly. 'Tell me about Katie, *cara*. Who is she?'

In the silent room the ticking of the cuckoo clock on the mantelpiece echoed the painful thud of Jess's heart. She felt as though she was standing on the edge of a precipice, but when she looked into Drago's dark eyes she knew suddenly that he would catch her if she fell, that she would always be safe with him. She thought of their wedding the previous day. He had gone to so much effort to make the day special for her, and when he had looked into her eyes while they had made their vows his tender expression had reassured her that she could have faith in him.

'You're holding her,' she said huskily. She gazed at the wooden figurine in his hand. 'Katie is my daughter.'

More shocked than he had ever been in his life, Drago forced himself to speak calmly. 'You have a child? Where is she? And who is her father?' His eyes narrowed on Jess's white face and the truth hit him as if he had been punched in the stomach. 'It's Loxley, isn't it?'

'He didn't want to know when I told him I was pregnant.' Jess's voice was a thread of sound. 'I was seventeen, alone, and terrified about the court case I was facing for the fraud charge. My social worker suggested that it might be best for the baby to be adopted and…and I agreed, because I didn't know how I would cope.'

Jess closed her eyes and so did not see the conflicting emotions that crossed Drago's face: anger at the man who had hurt her so badly, and a depth of compassion for Jess that made him pull her into his arms and simply hold her tight.

He stroked her hair, and the gentle caress calmed Jess a little. 'The baby was born on the fifth of April,' she said quietly, wanting to tell him everything now—needing to let out the pain she had lived with for so long. 'She was such a pretty thing. I'd never seen anything so perfect. I called her Katie because it was the prettiest name I could think of, and I took her home because I loved her more than anything in the world and I wanted to keep her.'

Tears slipped down her cheeks. 'I was living with Ted and Margaret by then, and they were so supportive. But I had no job or money. I loved my beautiful baby, but I knew that she needed more than I could give her. The couple who wanted to adopt her had tried for a baby for ten years and they were desperate to have Katie. They promised they would love her and give her the happy and safe childhood that I hadn't had. When she was three weeks old I cuddled her and kissed her one last time, and told her that I would never, ever forget her.'

The tears were falling harder now, and as Drago pulled her close she clung to him and her shoulders shook. 'And then I gave her to the social worker and that was the last time I saw my baby.'

'It's all right, *tesoro*, it's all right. Let the tears fall.' Drago did not know what to say. There were no words that would help. So he simply held Jess tight and laid a cheek that was wet with his own tears against her hair.

'Once a year Katie's adoptive parents send me a

photo of her,' Jess continued after a moment in a choked voice. 'They moved to Canada when she was a year old, and they live in a beautiful house in the mountains where Katie is learning to ski. She has a pony, and for her seventh birthday her parents gave her a puppy. They adore Katie, and I can see from the photos that she is happy. She knows she is adopted, and when she is eighteen she can decide if she wants to meet me. Every year I carve a new figure of her in the hope that if we do ever meet I will be able to show her that even though we were apart she was always in my heart.'

'Why didn't you tell me about her before?' Drago said quietly.

'I was afraid to,' she admitted. 'I was scared you would think badly of me because I gave my baby away, and maybe you would think I wouldn't be a good mother to our child.'

He shook his head. 'How could I think badly of you? I think you are incredible. Your decision to allow Katie to be adopted was utterly selfless. You put her best interests before your own happiness.'

He dropped his arms to his sides as an agonising realisation became clear to him. 'That
is the reason you agreed to marry me, isn't it?'
Drago said hoarsely. His throat felt as if he had
swallowed broken glass. 'You chose what you
believed to be best for our child over what you
wanted—which was the freedom to return to
your friends in London.'

'That's not true,' Jess said shakily, stunned by
the raw emotion in his voice.

'It *is* true. You admitted the day you went on
your own to Murano that you felt smothered and
missed your independence. You didn't tell me
about Katie because you didn't trust me—and I
understand, *cara*, I understand why you find it
hard to trust, but I hoped I had shown that you
could trust me.'

He brushed a hand across his eyes and grimaced when he felt his wet lashes. His heart was
being shredded and he was in agony. 'After what
happened with Loxley it's not surprising that you
felt you had no option but to accept my proposal
rather than struggle to bring up a child on your

own. And so you chose to sacrifice your personal happiness and marry me.'

His voice deepened. 'You once accused me of keeping you a prisoner, but now I am offering you your freedom. If you want to go back to England, you and the baby, I won't stop you. All I insist is that you will allow me to support you both financially. And of course I will want to visit our child often. But I have to tell you...' He took a harsh breath and felt his lungs burn. 'I have to tell you that the thought of living without you kills me.'

Drago looked into Jess's eyes, uncaring that there were tears on his face, unable to hide any longer how he felt for her.

'I love you, Jess. I didn't ask you to marry me just because of the baby. The truth is I want you in my life, always and for ever. But I was a coward and I didn't want to admit how I felt, so I used your pregnancy as an excuse to force you to marry me.'

He swallowed as he saw a tear slide down her cheek. 'Say something,' he pleaded.

'You really love me?' Jess was afraid to believe

him—afraid to believe in the happiness that was slowly unfurling inside her.

'I adore you. I desired you the second I laid eyes on you, and I think I fell in love with you when I caught you trying to escape from the *palazzo* by climbing down from a second-floor balcony.' Drago's patience snapped, and with a groan he pulled her into his arms and threaded his hands through her vibrant hair. 'Jess, *ti amo*! Please say you'll stay with me and let me love you and take care of you and our baby.'

Jess looked into his eyes and saw the intensity of his emotions, and she finally believed.

'I will,' she said softly. 'I love you with all my heart. You stormed into my life, and from that day I knew that you were the only man I would ever love.' She heard him catch his breath when he saw her love for him blaze in her green eyes. 'I would trust you with my life.'

'Tesoro...' Drago's voice cracked, but there was no need for words when he kissed her with such tender passion, such love, that Jess felt her heart would burst with happiness.

'My heart is your willing prisoner,' she whispered against his lips, 'and I never want you to set it free.'

'I've thrown away the key,' he promised as he swept her up and carried her to the bedroom, where he undressed them both and worshipped her body with loving caresses until she gasped his name.

He made love to her with exquisite care, and afterwards, as they lay content in each other's arms, he pressed his lips to her stomach, where his child lay, and told her that he was the happiest man in the world.

EPILOGUE

THE BABY WAS due in early January, but on Christmas Day, after a short labour, Jess gave birth to a son. They named him Daniel, and when she held him in her arms for the first time Jess felt a sense of peace that helped to heal the ache in her heart. She would always love and miss her daughter, but she knew that Katie was happy and adored by her adoptive parents. With Drago's re-assurance she had gradually came to terms with the devastating decision she had had to make when she had been a teenager.

'At least we'll never forget his birthday,' Drago said ruefully as he cradled his son in his arms and fell instantly and irrevocably in love with the tiny dark-haired infant.

His stress levels had gone through the roof when Jess had woken him at dawn and calmly informed him that her waters had broken. For a man used to being in control of every situation he had been riven with anxiety and frustration that he could do nothing to take away the pain of childbirth.

'You were amazing,' he told Jess, love and admiration blazing in his eyes. 'You *are* amazing. Have you any idea how much I love you, *mio amore*?'

'Show me,' she invited softly.

And he did. With a kiss that held tenderness and passion and the promise of a deep and abiding love that would last a lifetime.

* * * * *